T0162802

Scene 38 Take 3

L.J. Matarese

WestBow Press books may be ordered through booksellers or by contacting:

WestBow Press
A Division of Thomas Nelson & Zondervan
1663 Liberty Drive
Bloomington, IN 47403
www.westbowpress.com
1 (866) 928-1240

ISBN: 978-1-4908-2383-6 (sc)
ISBN: 978-1-4908-2384-3 (hc)
ISBN: 978-1-4908-2382-9 (e)

Library of Congress Control Number: 2014901428

Printed in the United States of America.

WestBow Press rev. date: 01/20/2014

To my amazing husband Phil.

Thank you for showing me what romance really is.

Prologue

This was supposed to be, the day every young girl dreamed about; her sweet sixteen party. For Laura Johnson, it was quickly turning into a nightmare. The beautiful cake sat untouched, and her mom moved to put the dripping ice cream back in the freezer.

She checked her watch for the tenth time. She could not understand it. "Mom, what time did you put on the invitations?"

"Don't worry about it sweetheart. I'm sure everyone's just running late."

"All fifteen party guests are forty-five minutes late? I'm not a baby anymore Mom. I'm sixteen," she said sarcastically. "I can handle the truth; nobody is coming to my birthday party. Who needs friends anyway when I have such a loving family?" She flopped onto the couch and hugged a pillow. Even her perfectly styled strawberry blond curls seemed to deflate.

Honestly, she was most disappointed that Andy Copeland hadn't come. She'd had a huge crush on him for as long as she could remember. "I guess he's too popular to come to my party."

Tears began to fall unbidden.

"I know it won't be the same but we can still make this day special. Wasn't there a movie that you wanted to go see that opens today? Dad and I would love to go see it with you and then we can go out for dinner afterwards."

The promise of dinner and a movie was enough to put a smile on Laura's face. Theater was her number one passion and had been since she could remember. It was her dearest wish to go to Hollywood and be part of the magic.

She took some comfort in telling herself that once she was a star her classmates would wish they had been nicer to her.

While her classmates sat at home not knowing what they wanted out of life, Laura already had a job and had started saving up money to move away as soon as she graduated from college.

Forcing her mind back to the present, she hugged her Mom and said, "Sweet! I have wanted to see *Hope for the Journey* since I saw the preview!"

It turned out to be the perfect way to celebrate her birthday. The movie more than made up for her disappointment about the failed birthday party, and the locket and purse that her parents gave her at the restaurant was enough to make her feel like an adult.

Chapter 1

Dallas Texas, 2000

Laura Johnson, would have given anything to feel like an adult right now. Now she felt very young and vulnerable even though she was twenty-three and on her way to Los Angeles California, to audition for her first movie. This had been her dream for as long as she could remember.

She had graduated from college a year earlier and spent that time working forty hours a week as a receptionist, at a small publishing house, and starring in four community theater productions in her spare time. Working and acting at the same time had been rough, but it paid off because she was discovered at one of those plays.

A talent scout had been sent to watch the production of *Oklahoma*, and he was impressed with her interpretation of Laurie. Two weeks later he called her and asked her to come out for a screen test.

She became more and more nervous as they approached the airport. Laura hadn't been away from home for longer than the two weeks she always spent at summer camp first as a camper and later as a counselor.

Since she lived in such a big city, there were a lot of good colleges within driving distance to choose from, so she hadn't even gone away for college.

Usually, Laura didn't have a problem expressing how she felt. However, at that moment, she couldn't say whether she was more nervous or excited. Everything was about to change.

"Good-bye Mom and Dad. I'll miss you," she said with a quiver in her voice that she coul.dn't quite control. As sad as she was to leave she couldn't wait to explore the world and see what she had to offer it in return.

"We'll miss you too," her mother, Jeanette, said trying to stay strong. "Don't forget to call us when you get into the airport. And don't forget to write to us so we'll have your address, and don't forget..."

"Mom! I promise I won't forget you. I could never forget you. You and Dad mean the world to me, and I wouldn't be where I am today without you."

"I know, I know, we love you too. Now, have a wonderful time in California, Laura. I know you'll do great, and I cannot wait to see what you accomplish."

"We're proud of you Laura; not everyone has the courage to follow their dreams," Bill told his only daughter with tears flowing down his cheeks. As he said this, he reached for his wallet. "I want you to use this to buy gas or a motel room or whatever you need. I love you Laura. You're going to do great in California."

Laura's eyes went wide as she counted out five hundred dollars. "Well, I definitely didn't see that one coming! Thank you both so much. I love you."

"We love you too. Just promise us you'll be careful. LA is a lot bigger city than Dallas."

She promised and gave both of her parents a hug and with reluctance to leave the familiar behind, took a deep breath and went to stand in line to board her plane.

"I can't believe that Laura is moving so far away. The house will feel so empty without her," Jeanette said no longer able to keep up the strong facade as they watched the plane taxi down the runway a few minutes later.

"There will be changes," Bill agreed. "Just remember the One who never changes. God will protect her, just keep praying for her like I know you have been and let God take care of the rest."

"I know. I just hate not being in control."

"You don't say? You sure fooled me."

That earned him a scowl and a playful swat. "Be serious."

"Why don't we pray for her right now?" he asked as he took her hands in his.

She nodded, and they both bowed their heads. "Lord, thank You for giving Laura this opportunity to use her talents for You. Please, protect her and give her discernment as she goes out for different parts and jobs, guide her on this journey…"

While Laura waited for her first flight to take off, she tried to think of something with which to distract herself. At the moment, she wasn't looking forward to flying alone.

She checked her itinerary for what must have been the tenth time. She had an hour layover and then another three hour flight. If everything went according to plan, she would be in California by late afternoon.

Unfortunately, things did not go according to plan. Due to stormy weather and the number of planes trying to land at the same time, Laura's first flight was delayed by half an hour.

She worried about missing her flight until she realized that her plane had landed in the same concourse as that of her next flight, and she only had to go to her gate.

She stepped into the gate area as they called her row to board the plane. *Lord thank You for being with me. I couldn't have done that without You.*

As Laura found her seat on the plane, she gave a sigh of relief. It wasn't until then that she realized how tired she was.

Ten minutes after the plane was in the air she was dead to the world.

When Laura woke up she was disoriented, but soon it all came rushing back to her. She couldn't stop the ear to ear smile that came, thinking about all the adventures she would have: living on her own for the first time, pursuing her dream, and getting to see all of the landmarks she had only dreamed about seeing. She especially couldn't wait to see the Hollywood Walk of Fame, Graumen's Chinese Theater and the Hollywood hill.

Laura was glad that she woke up when she did because, not five minutes later she heard the flight attendant say, "Please fasten your seatbelts and return your, tray to the upright and locked position. We will be coming into the airport shortly, all flight attendants, please prepare for landing."

She was almost in Hollywood. Just a few more hours and all her dreams would start coming true.

She had a window seat on this flight and looked down at the city through the clouds. When she was able to catch a glimpse of the buildings down below it reminded her how small she was. It was humbling to see how big the world was. She knew she could get so wrapped up in worrying about what was happening to her that, she completely forgot the rest of the world. It made her stop and praise God, that even with billions of people on the planet, God knew what happened to each and every one of them.

When the plane landed, she stepped off feeling the full gamut of emotions- excited to explore the world and afraid the same world would reject her. She reminded herself that it was most important what God thought of her. However, the comfort wasn't instantaneous.

Laura went to check into her hotel after renting an eight year old champagne Taurus, which the rental agency assured her was in perfect working condition.

She spent her first night in Los Angeles doing cold reads of as many monologues as she could find. Since she hadn't been sent a sample script she could only assume it would either be a cold read, or they would ask her to do a monologue she already had prepared.

Laura ordered room service so that she could keep working on preparing for tomorrow. If she didn't get the part, she knew it would not be from a lack of trying.

Chapter 2

The next morning Laura was up before her alarm. She made it a point to read her Bible before starting her day. She turned to her favorite Bible passage in Proverbs 3: 5-6 from the Message translation and read it out loud. "Trust God from the bottom of your heart; don't try to figure out everything on your own. Listen for God's voice in everything you do, everywhere you go; He's the one who will keep you on track." *Lord, please guide me today as I take the next step to get this part. If it's not meant to be, keep me on the right path. I choose to trust You.*

Since she had extra time this morning, she relaxed as much as possible. She was determined not to feel rushed for her interview with James Russell, an up and coming producer, was in thirty-five minutes and she only had a twenty-five minute drive.

Laura felt comfortable with how early she left until she backed out of her parking spot. She heard a loud crunch followed by a strange hissing noise and felt her spirits slump along with the car. This cannot be happening today of all days.

When she got out of her car, her fears were confirmed. The front tire on the driver's side was flat. She pulled out her cell phone to call the producer to explain what happened and why she would be late, but she couldn't find his business card.

Thankful that the car had a spare tire, and even more grateful her father had shown her how to change one; Laura went to work replacing the tire.

Well, here goes nothing, Laura thought to herself as she parked her car in front of the studio at ten fifteen.

She was about fifteen minutes late to her meeting, not bad considering she had to replace a tire. She prayed that James would understand.

"May I help you?" asked a girl who introduced herself as Ruth, the assistant director. "You look like you're lost."

"Yes. I'm here for an interview with James Russell," Laura said calling upon all of her talent as an actress to appear calm and confident.

"May I tell him who's here?"

"Laura Johnson."

"Okay, just follow me and I'll take you to him."

Ruth led her through a maze of hallways until they came to a corporate suite of offices. "Just knock before you go in; best of luck to you Cora."

"The name is Laura."

Ruth shrugged her shoulders and went on her way.

James Russell was a man in his mid-fifties and had salt and pepper hair that used to be all black. He had little patience for people who didn't keep their appointments. He was tired after a sleepless night, and if his last appointment didn't show soon, he would be late for a doctor's appointment. In fact, he ran the risk of missing it completely. His first impression did not improve when he heard a timid knock on his door. He managed to stay professional as he greeted his late appointment at the door and shook her hand, but he didn't offer her a seat. She wouldn't be staying that long anyway. "So you're Laura right?"

"Yes, sir," Laura said still nervous but not allowing it to affect her voice.

"Please, call me James. Everybody does." Before Laura was given a chance to reply he said, "I'm sorry that you wasted your time coming to California; however, a more experienced actress, who had a meeting with me before you came in, showed great work ethic by being here early. Now if you had been here on time we might have been able to work out some sort of deal. Unfortunately that was the last part that we needed to cast."

"James, please give me a chance to explain why I was late."

"This should be interesting. Okay, go ahead. What was so important that you couldn't be on time for this appointment? It makes me think you don't want to be in show business"

"I had a flat tire."

"I see," he said crossing his arms across his chest. "And why didn't you show some responsibility by calling me, or one of my assistants?"

Laura mentally cringed as she admitted, "I left your business card in my hotel room, and I didn't want to be any later than I had to be by running back up to my room."

"It's obvious you are not ready to handle the film industry. When you're ready to take this business seriously who knows, maybe there would be a place for you. Until then, have a safe trip back to wherever you call home."

With that Laura, walked out the door feeling foolishly.

She was in shock as she walked back to her car. *I knew I should have called and explained the situation with the car. He was right. I'm not professional enough. What was I thinking? Laura was on the verge of tears.* Then she had a calming thought. *Well, Laura, do you believe the prayer you prayed this morning or not? Didn't you ask God to keep you on the right track? Clearly he has something else in mind for you. It would have been almost impossible to develop as an actor under that kind of director.*

Chapter 3

When Laura found a restaurant for lunch, the place was packed. There after searching for five minutes, she finally found an empty table.

She was trying to decide what she was in the mood for, when she heard, "How is it that a beautiful young lady like yourself is all alone for lunch?" asked a tall man with wavy brown hair, blue eyes and a smile that revealed straight white teeth. "May I remedy that situation?"

Laura looked around the busy cafe and considering that there were plenty of people around and likely no empty tables she said, "How could I refuse such a charming offer?"

"So are you here for business or pleasure?" asked the tall stranger.

Laura wasn't sure why she went into such detail, but she did. "I don't know anymore. I had a meeting with a producer this morning, but I was late, so he told me to leave. So, now I have to figure out what to do from here. I'm sorry; you probably didn't want to know all that. Here I am venting about all my frustrations and you don't even know my name. I'm Laura Johnson."

"I'm Rob. Robert Lancing, but my friends call me Rob," his words came out in a jumbled mass.

An awkward silence fell.

Finally Laura asked, "So, what do you do Rob?"

"I am a director, producer, talent scout… you name it; I do it," Rob said flashing that million dollar smile again.

Just then a waitress came over to their table, so Rob missed Laura's look of surprise.

"I'm sorry that it took so long for me to get over to your table. It's been a hectic day. So what can I get for you, the usual?" she asked not paying any attention to Laura.

"Yeah, that sounds good."

"I'd like the house special," Laura said when the waitress started to walk away without even acknowledging her.

"Oh, I'm sorry. I'm so used to Rob being alone. I'll have that out to you as soon as its ready."

Rob blushed with embarrassment.

"So I take it you come here often?" Laura asked trying to rid herself of the feeling that everybody in this town ignored her.

"I come in two or three times a week. I usually sit at this table; that's why she knows me. So, where were we before we were interrupted? Tell me about your acting experience."

"Well, ever since I was five or six, I acted every chance I had. My neighbors and I would put on plays and in high school my friends asked me to help them make a commercial for a class I wasn't even taking.

"I commuted to Midwestern University and graduated with honors. There wasn't a production I didn't have some part, whether it was in front or behind the scenes. James Russell saw me in one of those productions, and he said he wanted to see more. I traveled all the way out here from Texas, but this morning I had a flat tire and the rest, as they say, is history."

"Are you going to stay in the area or will you be flying back to Texas?"

"I'm still trying to decide. Right now I don't have any other leads."

"Well, now you do. Come and audition for a part in one of my movies." Robert said hopefully.

"Why would you want me to audition? You don't have any assurance that I can act, and I might not be interested in the role you want me to play."

"Two things. First, that's why they call it an audition, for both of us to see if my movie would be a good fit. Secondly, I realize that James Russell can be a drill sergeant when it comes to selecting actors but I value his opinion, and if he thinks you're good enough to come out here and potentially be in one of his movies I don't think I'm taking that much of a risk." *Plus, I would love to see you again.*

"I'd love to say yes right now, but may I think about it and give you my answer in a day or two?"

"Of course; here's my business card. Call me, day or night."

"Thank you, for everything."

"You're welcome."

Soon after that Rob and Laura got their food.

Laura was surprised how easy it was to talk to this Hollywood big shot, but he seemed humble and grounded, the complete opposite of James Russell.

On the way back to the studio, Rob was surprised that he couldn't get Laura out of his thoughts. They had only spent an hour together.

Laura spent the rest of the night thinking and prayed about whether this offer was a gift from God. By all appearances, it was, but she just didn't want to rush into anything. She also did a substantial amount of research on the internet. As far as she could tell all of Rob's movies up to this point had been a family oriented and clean.

After having a light lunch the next day, Laura made her decision and called Rob.

He answered on the second ring. "Good morning, Robert Lancing speaking."

"Hi, Rob, this is Laura Johnson from lunch yesterday."

"Hi, Laura, I remember you. What can I do for you today?"

"I've decided to take you up on your offer and audition for your movie."

"I'm glad to hear that. If you come down to the studio, I will have everything set, up, and we can get started right away."

"Excellent. Just tell me how to get there, and I am on my way."

"Of course." Rob mentally congratulated himself on keeping calm because, on the inside, he was ecstatic. Something told him it wasn't a mistake that they sat down at the same table.

After getting directions from Rob, Laura hung up and wanted to dance. Her dream was still alive.

Chapter 4

Upon arriving at the studio, Laura was slightly nervous. The last time she auditioned, she was sure she was going to be cast she ended up with nothing. However, she reminded herself that all she could do was try her best and let the rest up to God. With this pep talk in mind, she started to feel better.

From the second she walked into the studio, the entire experience was exciting. Rob had his secretary waiting to show her to his office.

"Hello, Laura. Let's get your audition done, and then, if I like what I see, we can come back to my office and then my lawyer, and I will go over the standard contract. After that I'll give you a tour of the studio, a copy of the script, and things like that."

"That sounds good. Will I be reading with a partner or will it be a monologue?"

"There isn't anybody else around right now that could, but if you would be more comfortable having a reading partner, I would be happy to read opposite you."

"I would like that," she said trying not to sound too excited about it. *Man,this guy,is cute, and he's humble and sensitive too. Stay focused on the audition, the better you do, the better chance you have of seeing a lot of him*. The last thought made her smile enough that she started to relax.

She was glad that she had prepared for any audition scenario. She got the scene and looked at it for five minutes before telling Rob she was ready. She gave it her best shot, but her confidence wasn't high after meeting with James Russell.

Fortunately, Rob was more than confident that he had found the perfect actress. She looked like she belonged on a movie set.

They went back to Rob's office, and his lawyer was there to go over the contract with her.

She found that she didn't understand half of it because of the legal jargon, but Rob continued to be gracious and explained anything she didn't understand right away.

Laura was shocked when she read how much she would earn for her first movie.

Rob noticed her expression and asked her about it. "Is everything okay Laura?" he asked prepared to give her any sum of money she asked.

"I'm just shocked at how much you're going to pay me."

"Is it more or less than you expected?"

"More. I thought that since I wasn't a big name actress I wouldn't be paid this much."

Rob smiled. "Welcome to show business Miss Johnson. Now, would you like a tour of the studio?"

"I'd love a tour." *I can't believe this is happening! I'm really going to be in a movie!* She thought.

Laura thought she was going to get a crick in her neck from looking every direction for the duration of the twenty minute tour. Before today, she thought she would have to go back home. She understood that not everybody got hired so quickly. She was determined that she wouldn't take it for granted.

They ended the tour back at Rob's office. "Okay, here's your script and your rehearsal schedule. Rehearsal starts next week."

"Thank you for everything, Rob."

"You're welcome. I'm sure you'll do a fabulous job. I enjoyed reading with you. Considering how little time you had to prepare you did an excellent job. James Russell will regret his decision to let you slip through his fingers."

Laura found that she didn't want to leave with the handsome Robert Lancing paying so much attention to her. *Get a grip on yourself Laura. You don't know anything about him. He's just trying to build up your confidence and help you relax so you will act even better.*

"I'll see you next week then."

With a few more words, she left.

The rest of that day Laura couldn't stop praising God. She called her parents and told them all about how God had provided this work.

She couldn't help but think of her old high school classmates. What would they think of her now? She had a feeling that if she threw a party now everyone would come. The thought made her feel smug.

Reality didn't start to sink in until the next morning when she realized that she needed to start looking for a permanent place to stay. She couldn't stay in a cheap hotel forever.

She started her search by looking on the internet for houses listed in the area. Her jaw dropped when she saw some of the prices even for one bedroom houses. Eventually, she could afford such a place but right now all she had to go on was her savings until she received her first paycheck. In order to find anything affordable she discovered she had to rent an apartment in the suburbs and have a forty minute commute, assuming traffic cooperated.

It wasn't ideal, but she needed a place to stay and knew that the hotel room bill would add up fast.

By the end of the week, she was moved into a nice furnished apartment and began to settle into her new life.

Chapter 5

Laura intended to be at work a few minutes early her first day to prove to herself that she could be mature and responsible.

However, the night before she was so excited that she couldn't fall asleep. It wasn't until two thirty that she finally calmed down enough to go to sleep. So, when her alarm woke her up the next morning, she turned off the alarm, rolled over, and fell back asleep. Half an hour later she woke up and felt ready for the day.

She rolled over to turn off the alarm and realized she would never make it to the studio on time.

"This is just great," Laura fumed, "my first day on the job and I'm late." She rushed around the house trying to make herself look presentable before realizing that she would only be rehearsing today.

Laura spent the drive trying to stay calm. This time, she remembered to pull out her phone and call the assistant producer, Robin, to say that she was behind schedule "I'm sorry, I'm going to be about fifteen minutes late. My alarm didn't wake me up this morning."

"It's all right. You will find that schedules are relative around here but do try not to make a habit out of this." Robin said and abruptly hung up the phone.

The rest of the day went better than its rocky start. When Laura finally arrived at the studio, she met the rest of the cast and then they got right into the rehearsals. Laura wasn't the main character, so she had plenty of free time to sit in the dressing room or watch the rest of the cast rehearse.

By the end of the day, Laura was tired but completely content. She felt like a natural and found everyone in the cast to be friendly. Laura knew that there would be times that tempers would run high, but she was determined to enjoy every bit as much as possible.

After the rehearsal Rob, came over and complimented Laura's acting. "You were excellent today Laura."

"Thank you Mr. Lancing. I enjoyed it," Laura tried not to blush.

"Call me Rob. I'm glad that you're enjoying it."

Rob stayed quiet for a moment but made no signs of moving.

"Did you want something else?" Laura asked trying to be polite. She couldn't tell if she were supposed to stay or go.

Rob continued standing there, his mouth opening and closing soundlessly. Finally, he asked, "Laura may I buy you dinner tonight?"

"Are you asking me on a date?"

"Yes, I am," Rob said. *Oh man, this was a mistake. She'll never agree to go out with me I'm her boss.*

"I have always been told that dating your employer was a bad idea. Aren't there regulations about that?"

"I know, it is usually frowned upon but not enough that either of us would be fired over it. It happens more often than you would think. Something about you fascinates me. I want to learn what makes you tick. Will you give me a chance?" he would never admit it but she had been in his thoughts since the audition. This girl was different in the best sense of the word.

Laura thought for several minutes weighing her options. *On the one hand, she didn't know much about this man, and she knew she needed to be careful. On the other hand, she had never been on a date. Could she let this opportunity pass?* "Would it be all right if I met you somewhere? I have a rather long commute."

"Absolutely." Rob could have done a cartwheel but tried his best to keep his composure.

"Wonderful. Where did you have in mind?"

"Since you're new in town let's go to the restaurant where we met that way we are sure to both know how to get there," he said with another of his great smiles.

"It's a date," Laura said with a smile.

When Laura smiled, Rob felt like the room got a little bit brighter. He couldn't remember the last time he had seen such a genuine smile. His heart skipped a beat.

After discussing what time to meet they went their separate ways. *Did I just agree to go on a date with a Hollywood producer? I am so far out of my element. What should I wear?* Laura was distracted as she walked across the lot to her car. She was pulled back to the present when she realized that someone called her name.

"I just wanted to say hi, and ask how you liked your first day on set," said a girl Laura remembered seeing behind a camera

"Oh, thanks! It was excellent. I'm really enjoying it so far. Rob's a great director isn't he?"

"Yeah, about that, sweetie. That was the other reason I wanted to talk to you."

"What do you mean?" Laura asked butterflies in her stomach.

"He only asked you to be in the movie because he wants to date you. This happens every time he directs a movie. There's always one girl he singles out as his favorite. I just thought you ought to know before it was too late." Before Laura had a chance to reply, the girl had walked away.

Before Laura knew it, it was time to go meet Rob. She was more nervous now than when she agreed.

She managed to calm down and forget the other girl's words enough to get herself ready and go on her first date. It wasn't that she had never been asked out before, but she had never been interested in any of the guys who asked. It happened one of two ways: either she liked someone else at the time, or she knew enough about the guy who asked to know that he was not the type of person she wanted to have interested in her.

Laura pulled into the parking lot a few minutes before Rob. She spent the time praying she had made the right decision. Up until this point, she hadn't taken the time to consider the fact that she didn't know anything about Rob. She wasn't even sure how old he was.

Rob drove into the open parking spot next to Laura and waved. "I'm sorry; I meant to be the first one to get here," he said when they were both out of the car. "I, do, however, have a good excuse for being late." He reached back into his car and pulled out a beautiful bouquet of flowers, including three yellow roses.

"Well now, you are quite forgiven. If this is what I have to look forward to, please feel free to be late any time." Laura said with her sweetest smile. *Where did that come from, since when do you know how to flirt?* She pushed those thoughts out of her mind. She was determined to enjoy herself tonight.

Rob laughed. "All right, it's a deal. Shall we go in and get a table?" he asked as he offered his arm.

"We shall," Laura beamed as she took his arm.

When they walked in Laura was glad that it was quieter at night than it had been during the lunch rush.

When they chose a table, Rob was the perfect gentleman and pulled out her chair for her.

They asked the typical getting to know you questions while they ordered their food, and then waited for it to come. They asked about each other's families and where they grew up, and high school. However, a good portion of the questions involved movies in one way or another.

"If you could describe yourself as any character who would you be and why?" Rob asked.

Laura thought for a moment before saying, "Rob, can we talk about something before we get into these getting to know you questions?"

"Sure. Are you okay?"

"I'm not sure. That's why I want to talk to you about it. Why did you hire me?"

"I'm sorry?"

"I asked why you decided to hire me," Laura told him again.

Rob was still confused but said, "I hired you because, like I said, if you're good enough to be considered by James Russell, you're good enough to be considered by me, why do you ask?"

"It's just that there has been talk on set that you only hired me because you wanted to date me. Before I have dinner with you, I have to know if that's true or not."

Rob took a moment to answer. "It's true that I was attracted to you the moment we met, but I'm running a business too. I hired you because you can act. Anyone who says differently, is just jealous."

Laura nodded, looking satisfied. "Now, to answer your first question about whom I would play in the movie, I would have to say Dorothy from *The Wizard of Oz*, because I feel like I have also stepped outside of my world where everything is more colorful than I ever imagined it could be. I'm extremely curious about what movie character you think is most like you." After that, the conversation was a lot freer.

Rob thought for some time before answering. "I would have to say that I most relate to Peter Pan because even though I have a big important job I still feel like a kid."

"How old are you?" Laura asked, glad for the perfect lead in to a question she didn't know how to ask.

"I'm twenty-seven. I know you aren't supposed to ask a lady how old she is so if you would prefer not to say that's fine," he said with a grin.

Laura would have answered him but just then their food came and neither thought about it again.

"Do you mind if I say a prayer before we begin eating?"

"Not at all."

"Lord, I thank you for this night and ask that You would guide our discussion and bless this food that it would give us the strength and energy so we may continue to honor and glorify You. In Jesus name, amen."

"You're a Christian aren't you?" Laura said in amazement.

"Yes, I am."

"What a relief, I am too. Before you came this night I was sure I had made a mistake; because, I realized I didn't know anything about you or what you believed."

"I had the same thoughts on my drive over too."

Conversation was non-stop after that. Now that they knew they had the most important thing in common they connected on a whole new level. They didn't leave the restaurant until closing time.

Chapter 6

Dallas

Bill Johnson, an engineer, wanted nothing more when he came home than to kiss his wife and relax for the rest of the night.

When he walked into the house, Jeanette was more excited than usual to see him. Bill still loved flirting with his wife and asked, "So, did you just really miss me today?"

Jeanette shook her head no, then realized how that might make Bill feel. "I mean, yes, I did miss you today but that's not why I'm so excited you're home. There's a letter on the dining room table that I have been waiting to open since I got the mail this morning."

They sat on the couch to read the letter from Laura together.

Dear Mom and Dad,

I'm all settled in my small one bedroom apartment, so I decided to write you so that you have my address. It isn't very big, but with a little bit of decorating I'm sure it will be just perfect. The original part I came out here for didn't fell through. Then I went to lunch and met Robert Lancing a producer. He liked me so much that he told me to audition for him, and I ended up with the part! Robert is wonderful to work for, and I recently found out that he is also a Christian. God is definitely guiding me down a wonderful path. Well, that's all for now. I love you both. I hope you are both doing well.

Love, Laura

"It sounds like she's doing well," Bill said after reading the letter.

"Yes, it does. I am so glad that she got that other job!" Jeanette exclaimed.

"So am I. Although, part of me thought that she wouldn't actually be staying in Hollywood," when he saw the look that his wife gave him he added, "It wasn't that I thought she wasn't talented enough, but it's a tough career to get started."

"It just goes to show that all things are possible with God."

Bill nodded. "You are absolutely right."

Bill went into the family room to read the paper and Jeanette decided to call Laura.

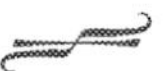

Laura was about to get ready for bed when her phone rang. She answered on the first ring wondering if it might be Rob. "Hello?"

"Hi, Laura. How are you?" Jeanette asked.

"Hi, Mom! I'm doing fine. How are you and Dad?" the feeling of disappointment only lasted a few seconds.

"We're good; we got your letter today. What happened with the other part? Are you disappointed?"

Laura took a moment to think about it then said, "No, I'm actually not disappointed at all. I've only been on set for a week, but I'm making a lot of friends and I'm learning a lot. I really like the producer. He's also a strong Christian and very sweet." She then told her mother the whole story of how she met Rob.

By the end of the story, Jeanette had a big smile on her face. Unless my ears deceive me, it sounds like Laura has a crush on Rob. She tried to concentrate on what her daughter was telling her, but she was also praying that God would bless Laura with a wonderful relationship.

Hollywood

In the next few weeks Laura developed something of a pattern. On the days, she had to be at the studio she would have dinner with Rob. Then, on the days she didn't work she would continue to find an endless supply of boxes that needed to be unpacked.

On her way into work one morning, she nearly ran into Cathy, one of the production assistants.

"Hey Cathy, how are you?"

"I'm good. How are you?"

"I'm all right."

"I keep meaning to ask you but for some reason I never remember. Would you come to church with me sometime? Rob told me last week that you were a Christian."

"You go to church? I'd love to go. I've missed going, but I haven't taken the time to find a good church in the area."

"We meet at Rob's house."

"What time does the service usually start?"

"It usually starts at 9:30. There are usually about twenty-five us there. There are five of us from the studio."

"I had no idea there were so many Christians on the set. Who are they?"

"It's Robert, myself, Sandy, Matt, and Jack. If you have any other questions feel free to ask."

"Thanks, I do have a couple of questions, but I'll just ask Rob."

"That's fine. We better get in, or Rob will come looking for us and ask what happened."

"I wondered what happened to you two ladies," Rob said, just coming on the scene.

"You know, if I didn't know better I would say that was scripted."

Laura and Cathy could not contain their laughter.

"I get the feeling that I missed something," Rob said with half a smile.

They tried to get themselves under control but failed miserably.

Rob just shrugged. "So glad you enjoy my presence, Laura."

Laura winked, and he was surprised at the butterflies in his stomach.

The day went well for everyone.

That night Laura wasn't talkative at dinner.

Rob mentally ran through the events of the day trying to figure out if he had said or done something stupid. Coming up blank, he finally asked, "What's on your mind?"

"Can I get directions to your house Rob?"

"You need directions to my house? Of course, you can but why do you need them?" Rob asked in confusion.

"I'd like to come to your house for church. Why didn't you ever tell me about it?"

"I'm sorry, I just never thought about it when you were around and when I did think about it, it was when you weren't around."

"So, it wasn't because you don't want me to come?"

"Not at all, I enjoy spending time with you, whether eating dinner, working together, or going to church with you. Now, let me do this properly." Rob cleared his throat dramatically and took Laura's hand in his. "Laura Johnson, would you go to church with me? I know it must be hard being away from your own church family but at least if you came with me you would know somebody."

"Wow. You really know how to apologize don't you. How can I say no to such an offer? I would be delighted to accompany you to church."

After that, the rest of the night went smoothly. Rob made no move to release her hand, and that was more than okay with her. Sometimes it still boggled her mind that she was sitting here, having dinner with a producer. Even more shocking was the realization that she felt like she was starting to fit in this world of show business.

Laura didn't remember ever smiling as much as when she was with Rob. Before she knew it nearly two hours had passed, and she was on her way home.

Conversation was comfortable and relaxed as Rob drove her home. Usually, Rob just dropped Laura off in the parking lot but tonight he walked her up to her door.

"Thanks for a wonderful night."

"You're welcome," Rob took Laura's hand in his and asked a question he had wanted to since the first date. "May I kiss you good night?"

Laura wanted to say yes, but she couldn't form any words so finally she just nodded yes. When they pulled apart they both had silly grins on their faces.

As much as Rob wanted to linger he forced himself to walk away with a whispered good night.

As Laura got ready for bed, she found everything she did was taking longer than usual because every few seconds she would stop and sigh in pure contentment.

Chapter 7

That Sunday, Rob found that he was more nervous than usual. He usually felt a twinge of nervousness before getting up to speak, but today was different. Now Laura Johnson was coming to church.

Rob found himself thinking about Laura a lot recently. He was not sure what his feelings were, but he did know that he wanted to get to know her better. Whenever he thought about their relationship becoming more permanent, he smiled. All he wanted to do was spend time with her, even if it was just a couple hours at a time. He decided right then that he would officially ask Laura to be his girlfriend today.

"Okay Rob, stop it. If you keep thinking about this, you're going to get even more nervous. If you're nervous you won't make any sense and then she won't want to come back again." He finally realized what he was saying and shook his head. "God gave you a message to speak so get out there and deliver it," he told himself.

With this pep talk, over, he went to the living room. Before he knew it, the small group of believers, was in his house, and it was time to begin the service.

Please give me peace, Father.

While Rob preached; Laura tried to focus on the message he gave but found it hard not to stare at him. However, once she got her mind focused on the real reason she was there she was inspired by what he said. He spoke about the importance of forgiving others by using a parable about a servant who had a huge debt forgiven; but, was unwilling to forgive another servant's debt.

Laura was humbled by the message. *I haven't done a good job with forgiving others. It's high past time I forgive my friends who didn't come to my sixteenth birthday.*

I really wanted Andy to be there though. I guess I always knew that he would never date me, but I would have gladly settled for being his friend. God, I don't know what Your plan was in all of that pain; but, if You were protecting me from worse pain by not dating Andy I thank You and trust You. I forgive you Andy. You owe me nothing.

Laura felt a wave of peace flood her soul as Rob gave the closing prayer. "Lord, as we leave here today let us not forget everything you have blessed us with, today and every day. Reveal your love to each of us in new ways. In Jesus name amen."

After the service everyone, stood around and talked. It took Rob several minutes to make his way over to Laura.

"That was a wonderful sermon Rob."

"Thank you Laura. What are your plans for lunch?"

"I planned to have some leftovers. Why?"

"I thought that we could go to Claire's for lunch. Would you like to join me?"

"I'd love to go."

"Great let's go."

Laura laughed. "Right now?"

"Yes. What did I miss?" Rob asked, confused.

"We, can't go yet. You still have guests."

"What?" Rob looked around and realized she was right. For a moment, he had forgotten that anybody else existed. "Oh! Hey, guys, can I ask a favor of you?"

"Sure," Matt replied for the group.

"Can the last person to leave, lock the door for me?"

"Sure thing buddy. Go on, have a good time." This again came from Matt.

"Thanks Matt. I appreciate it."

"You're welcome."

"Well, shall we go?" Rob asked turning to Laura.

"I guess so," Laura said, unsure about leaving when Rob still had company.

"Thanks again."

They all exchanged amused glances after Rob and Laura left.

After they had left, Cathy turned to Matt and said, "Well, it looks like you owe me a lunch Matt."

Matt laughed. "I guess I do. Where do you want to go?"

The rest of the group interrupted. "Why does he owe you a lunch Cathy?"

"What kind of wager did you two have?" someone else asked.

"We had a bet that Laura and Rob liked each other and that they would slip out of here as soon as possible. Matt thought Rob would wait around and be a good host, and I bet against him."

Five minutes later the group dispersed, and Matt locked up the door as promised. He turned to Cathy, "Shall we go my lady?" Matt asked offering her his arm.

"It would be my pleasure."

When they got in the car, Cathy looked over at him and said, "You don't actually have to take me out if you don't want."

"I know I don't. Cathy there's something I have to tell you. I made that bet with you because I knew that either way I would get to have lunch with you. I've liked you since, the first day we met three years ago. The entire time we worked on our first movie I wanted to ask you out, but I was a chicken. Then, when I found out we would be working together again, I knew I couldn't miss another opportunity like this. Will you go out with me?"

"I wish you would have asked me out during the first movie. I always felt like we connected well on the set too. But what changed that made you decide to take a chance after all this time?"

"I guess just seeing Rob and Laura together made me think that maybe costars could date each other. So, is that a yes or no on dating me?" He asked with a wink.

Cathy tried to feign nonchalance but didn't quite succeed. So instead of answering him directly she gave him a kiss on the cheek and said, "What do you think?"

They were both so caught up in their own little world that neither of them did a whole lot of thinking that night.

Rob and Laura's afternoon started with lunch at the cafe where they first met followed by a movie.

"You're not sick of movies?" Laura asked as they drove to the theater.

"I could never get sick of movies. Especially not when I get to see a movie with such a beautiful woman," Rob said.

Laura smiled and felt her face go red.

Rob reached for her hand and said, "I meant it when I said you were a beautiful woman. You have such a kind heart, and I know you would be willing to do anything for anyone. Since I met you, I have seen something special in you. Will you be my girlfriend?"

Laura's heart started beating faster. "Do I need to answer you right now or can I have some time?",

"Of course you may have time." Rob's heart sank. *She doesn't like me. I feel like a fool.* After a moment, he quietly asked, "Can you tell me a reason, or do you just need some time to get used to the idea?"

"Well, you might think this is an outdated reason, but I'd like my parents to meet you before I say yes, or no."

Rob laughed in relief. "I don't think that's an outdated reason at all. You want them to meet me to make sure that they approve. If they don't approve of us, you'd ask us to be just friends. Am I right?" he asked.

"That's it exactly. You wouldn't mind asking my parents?" Laura asked in surprise.

"Of course not. I think it's great that you love and respect your parents enough to do that. In fact, it makes me like you even more."

"Thank you, Rob."

"You're welcome. So, do you still want to watch a movie? Or would you rather do something else?" he asked sensing that they could use a change in subjects.

After thinking for a moment, Laura asked, "Can we go bowling instead of going to the movies?"

"I haven't been bowling in ages. I'd love to go. Do you have your own bowling shoes?" he asked.

"No, I don't do you?"

"No, we'll just rent some when we get there."

And off they went. They bowled two games and then Rob took Laura out for a casual dinner.

"Would you mind driving me back to your place so that I can pick up my car?'

"Sure. It has been a long day. You ready?"

"I am. Thank you for everything Rob. I will be calling my parents tomorrow."

"You're welcome. I'm glad to hear that."

Both were tired, so neither spoke much on the way back to Rob's.

When Laura finally got back into her car, she said a sleepy good night, and drove home with loud music on to keep her awake.

When she finally did lay her head down on the pillow, she went right to sleep.

Chapter 8

When Laura woke up, it was nine o'clock. She stretched lazily and thought how wonderful it felt to catch up on some sleep. Then as realization hit she scrambled out of bed and grabbed the first outfit she found. She was an hour late to work.

She decided to skip breakfast and grabbed her purse and headed out the door.

In her rush to get there as quickly as possible, she broke the speed limit. It took Laura a moment to notice the red and blue lights flashing in her rearview mirror.

She sighed very heavily, especially when she saw the amount of the ticket.

Finally, she was able to continue on her way; albeit, much more slowly.

She finally arrived and saw Rob pacing in front of the building.

The knot in her stomach grew.

"Hi, Rob," the apprehension was in her voice.

"What happened? I was getting nervous. I tried to call your house, but you didn't answer."

Laura was shocked to realize that all she heard in his voice was concern. "You're not mad at me?"

"No, of course I'm not mad I just want to know what happened."

"Well, last night all I could think about was how much I wanted to sleep. So I went straight to bed and forgot to turn on my alarm clock. I woke up at nine, so I grabbed my purse and headed out the door. I must have left my cell phone at home. I was speeding a little bit and got a ticket. I'm sorry Rob. Where is everyone? I hope that I didn't make you cancel a whole shoot. If I did, I'm sorry.

"No, we were able to shoot some of the scenes that you were not in. Go get into makeup, and I will see you in a bit, and don't worry I am not mad at you. These things happen. Come talk to me again, though, before the first scene."

Laura relaxed, somewhat, knowing Rob wasn't upset with her. As soon as she was ready to start the day she went and found Rob, by the coffee machine. "Let's go in my office so we can talk."

Rob motioned to his office chair and told her to sit down. "I've noticed that you are extremely hard on yourself and always expect people to jump on you if you make a mistake. Have I done something to make you think that I'm an angry person? Why are you so anxious?"

"No, it's nothing you've done. I just feel out of my element working on this movie. Everyone else is so much more experienced than I am. Besides that the reason I didn't get to work with Mr. Russell was because I was late that day."

"First of all, nobody thinks of you as inexperienced. I have watched you; you really know what you're doing, almost as if it's an instinct for you. Secondly, Russell is just uptight all the time. But, most importantly, I am so glad that Russell didn't hire you because, if he had I might never have gotten to meet you, You mean so much to me, Laura."

"Thanks, Rob. When I'm thinking clearly, I'm honestly glad

that Russell didn't hire me. Thank you for believing in me when I wasn't even sure I believed in myself. You're the best."

After talking to Rob, Laura was able to relax for the first shoot of the day. That night instead of going out Laura went home so that she could call her parents at a decent time. For a moment, Laura thought it would go to the answering machine, but her Mom picked it up on the fourth ring.

"Hello?"

"Hey Mom, is Dad home too?" she asked without preamble.

"Sure. Do you want to talk to him?"

"I kind of hoped to talk to both of you together," she replied.

In just minutes both, her parents were on the phone.

"Hi, Dad. How is work going for you?"

"Hi, it's going fine. Are you okay? It's not often that you want to talk to both of us at the same time," her father said.

"I'm sorry. I didn't mean to make you worry. I wanted to ask you guys if you would come visit me?"

"Visit you? Well, of course we would love to, but why do I feel like there's something you're not saying?" Bill asked.

"Yeah, you see, I want you to meet someone. His name is Robert Lancing. He's the one that hired me after I lost the part with James Russell," she explained.

"Why do you want us to meet your boss?"

Laura sighed. *Here goes nothing.* "Well, we have been spending a lot of, time together recently and, just last night Rob officially asked me to be his girlfriend. I didn't say anything one way or the other. I told him that I wanted the two of you to meet him first. So will you come?" Laura asked hopefully.

"I think we could come; but why didn't you tell us about him before? It might not, be that easy to get tickets last minute like this."

"I guess I always think that a guy likes me, and I've ended up being wrong so many times I was afraid to hope again."

"I understand. Your father and I have some vacation time that we can take, but it's going to be about two weeks before we can come. We can't just take off without notice," Jeanette said.

Laura became animated. "I can't wait to see you; I'm sorry but I'm getting another call can I call you right back?"

"No problem. We'll call you when we book the tickets."

"Sounds wonderful. Love you."

"We love you too Laura. Be safe and have fun. Bye."

"Hello?" she answered her incoming call.

"Hey Laura, this is Rob."

"Hi Rob. How are you?" Laura asked.

"I'm good. How are you?" he asked warmly.

Laura did not even trying to contain her excitement as she said, "I'm great. My parents are coming. I was just talking to them before you called."

"That is wonderful. Will you go to lunch with me tomorrow?"

"Sure. I'd love to. What time?" she asked.

"Let's say twelve thirty."

"That sounds good. I'll be looking forward to it."

Once she got off the phone she called her parents back.

"Hi Laura, I just got off the phone with the airline. We are arriving in Hollywood in two and a half weeks. We'll fly in on a Friday. I can't wait to see you," Jeanette said with excitement.

"I'm glad that you're able to come. How long can you stay?" Laura asked hoping they would be there at least four days so they could visit her church.

"We'll stay until sometime on Tuesday. I can't remember what time the flight is."

Laura paused for a moment. "You know that I'll have to work while you're here right?" Laura asked.

"I understand Laura. Do you think that we could watch you film one day?"

Just then Rob pulled into the driveway.

"I think that you should ask Rob when you meet him."

Laura's mom tried to protest. "Laura, I can't talk to a major producer, I would be too scared."

Laura, however, wasn't listening. She greeted Rob at the door and handed the phone to him. When, Rob held the phone to his ear, he heard, "... so you see it doesn't make sense."

Rob didn't know what to say, so he just said the first thing that came to mind, "May I help make sense of something for you, ma'am?

"Who is this? Where is my daughter?"

"I'm Robert. Who are you?" he asked in total confusion.

"I'm Jeanette. Now you better let me talk to Laura," there was a slight pause then, "Wait a minute. You said your name was Robert?"

"Yes ma'am," Rob replied, still completely in the dark.

"You wouldn't by any chance be Robert Lancing, would you?"

"Yes, I'm Robert Lancing. Do I know you?" he asked without a clue.

Jeanette acted like she didn't hear him.

"Laura. Oh boy. She really got me this time. Rob, I'm Laura's mom."

Everything finally fell into place for Rob. "Why did she do that?"

"Well her father and I are traveling out there soon. I had something to ask you, but I was a chicken," Jeanette replied.

"So what was it?" Rob asked out of curiosity.

"Would it be possible for us, me and my husband that is, to watch you shoot the film?" she asked knowing that her words weren't coming out right.

"Of course you may."

"Are you serious?"

"Sure.."

"Great. Can I talk to Laura for a couple minutes?"

"Sure, on one condition."

"What's that?" she asked on a chuckle.

"Don't be too mad at Laura."

Jeanette laughed.

"Here's Laura."

"Thanks Rob."

"You're welcome."

"What was the meaning of that, young lady?" Laura's mom asked in fake outrage.

Laura tried for the innocent approach, of, "I was only trying to get you and Rob to like each other, that's all. I didn't want the first time you met to be awkward."

Jeanette just laughed and said, "Now, how about getting your father to like him?"

"Has he said anything to you about Rob?"

"No, he hasn't said anything."

"Hey, Mom as much as I'd like to keep talking I have to go now. Rob and I are going out for lunch."

"All right, I'll talk to you later. I love you."

"I love you too. Bye Mom."

"Bye," Jeanette said still chuckling about the phone call she had just had. *Thank You Lord, for bringing someone into Laura's life who understands that girl's sense of humor.* As much as Jeanette wanted to be annoyed at Laura all she could do was laugh.

Chapter 9

"I don't know when I've enjoyed a phone conversation more." Rob exclaimed when Laura was off the phone. "She was a good sport about it."

"I knew that she would never ask you herself," Laura said explaining her actions.

"You want to know something?" Rob asked all laughing gone.

"What is it?"

"You're a good actress, most girls I know couldn't have handed me the phone like you did and not even smile." After pausing he added, "I think that you would be perfect for a part in my next movie." He hadn't planned on saying anything yet because one of the scenes involved a kiss, and he was not sure how that would make her feel.

"Do you think so?" Laura asked in surprise.

"Why do you sound so surprised?" Rob asked.

"Well, when you said I'd be perfect you got a weird look on your face," Laura said feeling unsure herself.

"Well, I hadn't planned to tell you yet."

"Why not?" Laura asked.

"I wanted to wait until your parent got here that's all."

"Why?" Laura asked voicing her only thought.

"Well, I'd be acting in it as well."

"Would that be so bad?"

"Well, if we were dating it wouldn't be bad at all; but, if not it could be potentially awkward."

"Why is that? I don't see why we couldn't at least be friends. Besides we're both professionals. I don't see a problem."

Rob could tell that subtlety wouldn't work. "It would be awkward because, we would be kissing. And if we almost date and then don't, I think it would be hard to kiss you and not want more than friendship."

"I see, yes, that could be awkward. I hope that doesn't happen. You're a kind and caring person. Any girl would be lucky to be with you."

Rob blushed. "Laura?"

"Yes, Rob?"

"Why hasn't any man swept you off your feet?"

"Oh, I just haven't had good timing with guys. Either I didn't like them, or they didn't like me; it just never worked out, or went anywhere. My first crush was the worst."

"Why, what happened?"

"Well, it all happened in junior high and high school. I liked this guy in my class, but he didn't like me. His name was Andy, and I thought he was the cutest guy in the whole school. He liked me as a friend but nothing more. We grew up together, but something happened when we got into high school. He became popular, and I didn't. By our senior year, he started dating somebody else and made fun of me to boot." Laura sighed. Even though she had forgiven Andy it was still hard to think about him. Wanting to escape her own thoughts she asked, "So what's your story? There must be a lot of disappointed girls out there."

"I don't know. I didn't like any of the girls in my high school. I never dated much. Besides, drama wasn't considered to be the cool club. My problem was I always liked people outside of my social order, if you will. I just didn't think any of the girls would be interested in me I guess. I use to have very low self-esteem. I was so busy with productions I wouldn't have had time to date anyway. So, it worked out for the best."

"What changed, to make you so much more confident? I would never have guessed that you had self-esteem issues."

"I think it happened when I went to college and started learning about the movie industry and found out that I was good at it. It made me realize that doing something you're passionate about is infinitely more important than being well liked by a group of kids who barely like themselves."

Rob and Laura realized at the same time that they were still sitting in Laura's driveway.

"Are we going to go anywhere?" Laura asked on a laugh.

"Yes, are you hungry?" he asked.

"Very."

"Okay, let's see if we can get out of the driveway this time," Rob said on a chuckle.

This time they did. They got back around 2:30. "Thanks for lunch Rob."

"You're welcome. I'll call you later."

"Okay.."

Chapter 10

That evening Laura's mom called to work out the details of their visit. It was only three days until her parents were scheduled to arrive.

Around six o'clock, she got another phone call.

"Hello?"

"Hello, Laura?" asked a vaguely familiar voice.

"Yes. Who is this?" Laura asked.

"This is Greg, from the studio."

"Oh, I knew your voice sounded familiar. What's up?"

"Will you go to dinner with me tonight?"

"You do know that Rob and I have been spending a lot of time together don't you?"

"I just need somebody to talk to me."

"Okay. I guess I can have dinner with you. Can I meet you somewhere?"

"Yeah, that's fine. Do you know where Claire's is?"

"Yes, I know where that is."

"Can you be there in half an hour?"

"I think so."

"I'll see you then."

With that, both hung up the phone. Greg was second-guessing himself, and Laura began to wonder what she had done.

Greg and Laura pulled up at the same time.

"Impressive timing," Laura said with a laugh.

They didn't talk again until after they had been shown to a table.

"Thanks for coming on such short notice."

"You're welcome. What's on your mind?" Laura asked wondering what this was about.

Just then, their waitress came to ask what they wanted to drink. Laura ordered water, but Greg ordered a beer.

By that time, Greg was ready to talk.

"I've been watching you since you came here. There's something different about you. What is it?"

"I'm different because I've accepted God's son and do my best to live the way He wants me to."

"So you're a... what a Christian?" he asked having trouble saying the last word.

"Yes, I am."

"Most Christians I know always preach at me and then go out do exactly the opposite of what they tell me to do."

"Well, I'm not into preaching. If someone asks for advice I will gladly share with them but I never shove ideas down anyone's throat."

Greg knew that he had a choice to make. Either, he could ask Laura what this whole Christian business was all about, or he could let the moment pass. *Why did you ask to meet her if you didn't want this question answered?*

Just then their waitress came back with their drinks.

"Are you ready to order?"

"Can you come back in a couple minutes?"

The waitress nodded and walked away.

Laura had a feeling that talk of spiritual things had passed; she was wrong.

"How can you serve a God who lets his children suffer? I thought he was supposed to be a loving God."

"He most certainly is a loving God, I have no doubt about that. We aren't living in the world God intended us to live in. When Adam and Eve disobeyed God by eating the fruit that would show them the difference between good and evil, they were saying that they didn't trust God, their Creator, to know what was best for them.

"But one of my favorite things about God is that He always gives us a chance to turn back. But Adam and Eve rejected that too. This separated them from God, and God knew that if they ate from the tree of life they would live forever in that separation from Him. That's why they were thrown out of the Garden of Eden. When they left the perfection of the Garden, there were consequences that were, passed from generation to generation. That's why bad things happen. It's not that God wants them to happen, but it's the reality of the world we live in."

"Well, I certainly haven't ever heard it put like that before. He probably wouldn't want me though. I've rejected Him way too many times to think that He would want anything to do with me."

"I don't believe that for a second. The Bible says that God is not willing that anyone should perish. Here," Laura said digging through her purse. "A friend of mine from high school recently sent me this poem. I think you should read it."

Greg picked up the paper.

The Journey

Bethany Rogers

Today I met a man
Who opened up his door to me.
He asked me to have supper.
I said, "No I am looking for direction and don't have time."
He asked me to reconsider;
I thought for a minute and then said,
"I really need to go".
He asked if he could go along, as well.
I refused his offer of companionship.
He bid me farewell and said
"Please come back when you are done."
I went on my way and at first it was fun,
But then I saw the road and got a bad feeling.
I realized how strong and nice the man had been,
So I ran back and was about to knock, but the door opened.
He welcomed me in and fed me.
I asked him to go on the journey with me.
He agreed and off we went.
We started on a different path, and it looked scarier.
I started to question him, but he said that he would be with me.
So I trusted and we went on.
The journey was very rough,
But he carried me when it got too bad.
And then my eyes were opened;
It was Jesus holding me.
My life has never been the same since I asked Jesus to go on a journey with me.

"Normally what you said would have set me on edge, but it did make a lot of sense when you explained it that way." Suddenly Greg realized that he started drumming his fingers on his glass, one of his nervous habits. He had always wondered how anyone could believe in God, let alone try to have a relationship with Him. "So, how does it work?"

"How does what work?" Laura asked patiently.

"If I was thinking about becoming a Christian how would I go about it? Do I have to be in church when I make that choice?"

"All you have to do is admit that you messed up and need God to forgive you for your sins. Then thank Jesus for dying on the cross and raising again on the third day to set you free."

"Do I have to say it out loud?" He asked, feeling self-conscious. He had no idea how to pray. And not knowing how to do something was a new feeling for Greg; he didn't like it. In his earnestness to find the truth, he leaned forward on the table.

Unbeknownst to Laura, at that moment Rob walked into the restaurant and saw the two of them sitting together.

"That isn't a requirement." Laura said kindly.

"I don't know if I'm willing to make that decision right now."

"Just know that God always accepts us even if we're not willing to accept Him."

Greg nodded and just as quickly as the conversation about God had started it ended. "How do you like being an actress?"

"It's exciting. Is this your first movie?"

"I was an extra in a movie but I didn't have any lines. So, what sounds good to you?" he asked, changing the subject.

"Meatloaf sounds good to me. What are you going to have?"

"I think I'll have steak and a baked potato."

They ate their meals with discussion going to all different topics.

Although Laura paid attention to the conversation, she was also praying for Greg. Specifically that something she said had made a difference in his life. Part of the reason that she wanted to be a Hollywood actress in the first place was so that she could be a witness to her costars. God certainly had answered a lot of her prayers recently. She went to bed after reading the Bible, and was out just minutes after her head hit the pillow.

Chapter 11

The next morning Laura woke up on time.

When she got to the set, Rob seemed frustrated with her. She thought that it strange, but told herself he was worried about meeting the deadline for the movie.

He seemed more like himself on Sunday, but on Monday he was in a bad mood again.

Laura didn't know how to respond to this, so she left right after work.

That afternoon, Rob, decided to call Laura and ask her to dinner.

He was relieved when she answered on the first ring.

"Hello?"

"Hi Laura, will you go to dinner with me tonight?"

"Sure, Rob..." she said hesitantly.

"Yes Laura?"

"Can you tell me what's bothering you? You haven't been yourself the last couple of days. Are you feeling okay?"

"Yeah, I'm fine," he said, unconvincingly. "Why do you ask?" he suddenly wished that he didn't hide his emotions so much. But, every time he thought about Laura and Greg he became angry again.

"You have been upset with me for the last two days. If you tell me what has you mad, we can work through it."

"Can we talk about that at dinner tonight?"

"I guess so. What time are you picking me up?"

"Can you be ready in an hour?"

"I think so."

"I'll see you in an hour."

Seconds later both hung up the phone.

"That was odd," Laura said to herself. *I wonder what I did that made him so irritable today, everything seemed fine last night.*

However, she didn't have time to speculate.

That night, on the way to dinner neither, spoke. Rob tried not to be mad at Laura, and she tried to figure out what was wrong.

They didn't start talking until they ordered their drinks.

"Laura, will you help clear something up for me?" Rob asked, trying to speak in a normal voice.

"I'll try to," she said.

"Now, maybe it was my imagination. Were you on a date with Greg on Friday?"

"No, Rob. I was not on a date with Greg this Friday night or any other night. I'm hurt that you trusted me so little," she replied disappointment evident in her eyes.

"What do you mean?" he asked knowing full well what she meant.

"I mean that you trust me so little that, without talking to me, you immediately thought that I was going out with him. Why would

I ask my parents to meet you if I was going out with somebody else?" Laura asked. "Just so you know, the reason he asked to meet with me was so we could talk about what it meant to be a Christian."

"You're right, Laura. I've behaved like a jerk. I guess it made me think back to high school and how the people I cared the most about didn't return my feelings. Can you forgive me?" he asked, feeling ashamed.

"I forgive you Rob." A sudden thought came to mind, and a grin spread across her face. If she weren't in public, she would have squealed.

"Well, that's the biggest smile I've seen in a while. Have I told you recently how beautiful your smile is?" he asked trying to regain some almost-boyfriend points. His efforts went unnoticed.

"I just remembered that my parents are flying in tomorrow!"

"Wow! Time sure has gone quickly. Will you meet them at the airport?"

"How would I be able to do that?"

"Didn't you read the bulletin board?" Rob asked.

"No. Why?"

"I cancelled the shoot," Rob replied.

"Why?" Laura asked again.

"My parents called and said they are coming."

"What if your parents don't like me?" Laura asked feeling nervous.

Rob wasn't given a chance to reply.

The food they had ordered finally arrived.

"Don't worry about it Laura. My parents will love you."

"I hope so."

They talked for another hour. By the end of the night, Laura felt much more relaxed knowing that Rob wasn't angry with her anymore and excited to see her parents the next day.

Chapter 12

The day that Laura had been anticipating finally arrived. Her parents were coming, and if the arrival board was accurate, their plane was going to be on time. She decided that the best way to surprise her parents was to wait at baggage claim.

Rob, however, decided not to surprise his parents. The two of them went their separate ways. Laura went off to baggage claim, and Rob stayed by the arrival board where he and his parents had talked about meeting.

For the last leg of their journey, both sets of parents would be on the same plane.

Laura got to baggage claim none too soon. Just five minutes after she got there she saw her dad coming toward her. She waved, but he didn't see her; he walked with his head down focused on his cell phone. So, she went about it another way. She would help her dad with the luggage.

"Excuse me, miss. That is my bag. Not yours." Bill said as he saw a hand reach for his suitcase.

"I understand that it is. Welcome to Hollywood, Dad!" she exclaimed.

Bill was speechless for only a moment.

"Laura? Is that really you? This is quite a surprise. Didn't you have to work?" he asked after he hugged her.

"I've missed you dad. I'll explain everything when mom gets here," Laura replied with a laugh. Where is she?"

"She needed the restroom. We agreed to meet here. How are you?"

"I'm good. Was that your only suitcase?" Laura asked.

He didn't get a chance to answer. Laura's mom was only a few yards away. Her reaction was much more intense than Bill's.

Unlike Bill, Jeanette walked with her head up and saw her from twenty yards away. Not caring that she was in public, Jeanette gave a shriek of surprise and ran to her daughter. "Laura? I thought you had to work!" She exclaimed and gave her daughter a big hug.

"Hi, Mom, I'll tell you about it later. How was the flight?"

"It was fine."

"Are you hungry?" Laura asked, knowing how neither of her parents liked the nuts that most airlines served.

"Yes," they both answered.

"Would you mind meeting Rob before we go eat? I made spaghetti."

"We would love to meet him now," Bill said.

Laura added as almost an afterthought, "It turns out that Rob's parents came in for a surprise visit and Rob is here waiting for them at the arrival board."

They walked in relative quiet, simply enjoying each other's presence.

"Mom, Dad, I'd like to introduce you to Robert Lancing. Rob these are my parents Bill, and Jeanette."

"It's nice to meet you both," he said holding out his hand.

"It's nice to meet you too," Bill said giving Rob's hand a firm squeeze.

"And, I'd like for you to meet my parents, Jill and Bob Lancing."

After another round of handshakes, they all agreed to have dinner at Laura's house. Rob and Laura had driven to the airport separately, so it was decided that they would split up, and meet up again at Laura's house.

There was little conversation on the way to Laura's car. The ride to her apartment was another story.

"So how did you get off work Laura?" Bill asked.

Laura became uncorked. She told her parents all the details of the last couple days. She ended up saying, "So was it a good surprise or a 'Why in the world would she do that?'"

"Of course it was a good surprise. But, don't do it again. I nearly fainted when I saw you," Jeanette joked. "So what time will Rob and his parents be here?" she asked changing the subject.

"I'm not sure. I'll have to call Rob this afternoon." That night they spent time catching up on each other's lives, around four o'clock Laura's parents took a nap.

She decided to take the opportunity to call Rob.

"Hello."

"Hi, Rob."

"Hi Laura, how are you?"

"I'm fine. How are you?" she asked back.

"I'm pretty good."

"Good. What time are you and your parents coming to dinner tonight?"

"I don't know. When do you want us to come?"

"How about you come at five-thirty, and we'll try to eat at six. Does that sound good?"

"Yeah, that sounds good to me."

They talked for another few minutes, but then Laura needed to start supper.

"I'll see you later Laura."

"Okay, have a good night."

Soon after Laura got off the phone, Jeanette came to the kitchen to talk to Laura. "So how do you feel about Rob?"

"I don't know. I know that I like Rob more than I've liked any other man. But, I don't love him. I know that your input is valuable. If you and Dad have any objections, I want to hear them."

At Rob's house, he and his parents had a similar conversation. Sitting at the kitchen table with his Mom, enjoying homemade chocolate chip cookies Jill asked, "So how serious are the two of you?"

"Well, we really haven't known each other long enough to be too serious but I like her a lot. I know that I'm not in love, but I care deeply about her. She is one of the kindest, prettiest, funniest girls I have ever met. I know that you barely met her, but based on first impressions, what did you think of her?" he asked hesitantly.

"I think that she seemed to be very nice. I'm sure that tonight will be a fun time." Jill said a smile lighting up her eyes. Her predictions were correct. They all had a wonderful time. They laughed most of the way through dinner.

"When I saw Laura sitting there at the table all I could think was that I had to talk to her. I have never been more grateful for a busy restaurant than I was that day. I have no idea how I would have met her if I hadn't sat down at her table."

"I thought you were bold," Laura admitted with a smile.

"I wouldn't have been that bold," Bob said with a laugh. "Your Mom was actually the one to ask me out first."

Jill laughed and said, "Hold on a second. That isn't exactly true," Jill said when the table erupted into laughter. "I only asked him if he would go to a movie with me and my family. We didn't even hold hands."

Bob wasn't ready to give up that easily. "That just meant it was a group date. Besides, don't you remember we shared popcorn that night? Our hands met several times in that bucket of popcorn."

Jill said nothing but leaned over and gave Bob a kiss.

Laura asked her parents, "It's your turn. How did you guys meet? Was it love at first sight?"

Bill and Jeannette looked at each other and laughed. "Are you going to tell the story or do you want me to tell it?" Bill asked.

"I never get tired of hearing you tell the story. Why don't you?" Jeanette suggested.

"Well you see, I had my eye on Jeanette since the eighth grade. She was in the choir, and I thought she looked like an angel. And when she sang her solo I was convinced she was. We were really good friends, but I was always too nervous to ask her out. Then one summer, she and I went horseback riding and the sun was shining in her hair like a halo, and I knew that I had to ask her out."

"So, Dad, you were in the friend zone?" Laura asked.

"Yes, I was. I really don't care though. Your mother was worth waiting for those two years. In fact, I would have gladly waited another two years."

"So, tell me Rob, what is it like to live in Hollywood and work with such big names?"

"It is hard work, but we have a lot of fun every day. Outtakes are always funny, but what always makes me laugh the most is when we work with a green screen, so everybody is dressed in these skin tight green suits called Chromakey. It's interesting to see how they interact with their surroundings that they can't even see. It's quite impressive."

"I want to show you something. Stay here," Jeanette commanded.

Everyone in the room looked at each other with confusion.

"I cleaned out the attic recently and put this in my purse. This is a poem that you wrote in elementary school."

"Oh boy, this should be good," Laura said with a groan.

Rob put his arm around Laura's shoulders. "I'm sure it will be amazing because you wrote it."

"You're sweet to say that but maybe you should reserve your judgment until after you've read it."

Fishing
Laura Johnson

Fishing with dad
Is never bad,
We have much fun
Out there in the sun.
We go out quite early,
Sometimes feeling surly;
When we find a lot of fish
We keep them to put in a dish.
We go out on his boat
And catch fish, but we never gloat
About who caught how many,
Once I caught a fish that had a penny.
At noon, we have lunch,
And we eat grapes that come in a bunch;
Then it's back to the poles
Until, on the line, a fish pulls.
Then we hurry to crank the spinner
Hoping we will catch it for dinner,
Around five o'clock

We head for the dock.
Yes, fishing with dad
Is never bad,
Then when we get home, and after all is said
We go, even though it's early, to bed.

"Wow that brings back memories. I remember that my teacher had us write one each year."

They talked for another half hour before going to bed.

Chapter 13

The next morning both Rob and Laura were feeling tired, and both of them agreed that they could both use a couple more hours of sleep. However, they had a job to do. Today they were filming the climax of the movie, so they couldn't afford to be tired. It wasn't until Laura drank her third cup of coffee that she started to wake up. They were able to make it through the day without too many problems.

"So, what did you think of my parents?" Rob asked after work. They were finally able to talk.

"I thought they were wonderful. What was your impression of my parents?" Laura asked back.

"I thought that they were nice. Your Mom made me laugh. Do you and your parents have a plan for the rest of the week?" Laura asked.

"No, not really; they've already been here several times already. Have you decided what you're going to do yet with your family?"

"I think that, for the rest of the week, we're planning to see some of the sights and then come back and talk late into the night.

It mainly depends on what my parents want to do. They have never been here, so there's a lot of places I want to take them."

"Laura, this is sort of out of the blue, but, now that your parents have met me and seem to like me, have you decided if you'll be in my next movie?"

"I still need to think about that Rob. I mean I've always wanted to be a professional actor, but I don't want to rush into anything. I just need to think and pray about it some more."

"No problem. Take all the time you need," Rob said, giving her a kiss.

They didn't talk a whole lot longer, because they both wanted to get home to their parents.

However, Laura might not have been so excited had she known what awaited her.

"Hi, Dad, is everything okay? Have you been crying?" Laura asked in some alarm when she saw her Dad, with blood shot eyes, sitting on the couch and staring off into space.

"Your Mom had to be taken to White Memorial Medical Center," he replied not wasting any time.

Laura stopped dead in her tracks. "What? What happened? Is she all right?" she asked anxiously.

"I don't know what happened. She just collapsed on the floor. I called an ambulance right away," he replied.

"Well, why aren't you there? What if she wakes up and nobody's there?" she asked surprised by her own anger.

"I figured that if neither of us was here you'd be even more scared. Let's go right now."

Laura grabbed her purse and was in the car in record time. As she drove to the hospital, she called Rob and asked him to meet them there.

It was the longest forty-minute ride of Laura's life. When she realized they would have to go close to the studio she snapped at her Dad, "Why didn't you just call me at work? You could have been with Mom, and I could have had a head start on joining you!"

"I wasn't exactly thinking clearly just then."

Laura ran from the parking lot to the reception desk and demanded, "Where have they put Jeanette Johnson?"

"I'm sorry, only family members are allowed information on patients."

"I'm her daughter. And this is my Dad," Laura said. "Please, we just want to know what's going on," she said slightly calmer.

While this exchange, occurred, Rob came on the scene.

"Laura?" Rob didn't know how to act. He didn't know whether to hold her or what.

The decision was taken from his hands. When she saw him, she walked into his arms.

"Rob."

Laura clung to Rob afraid of what might have happened to her Mom. She wanted her Mom to be there when she got married and had kids. She wanted her to get to know Rob better. What if she had hurt her head when she fell and couldn't remember her and Dad? Her Mom just had to be okay. There was simply too much left for her to do.

Eventually, Rob broke through her thoughts when she heard him praying for Jeanette.

Laura turned back to her dad.

"Did you find out anything?" Laura asked.

"They have her stabilized. She is in a room on the third floor."

Without any more conversation, they proceeded to room 309. Laura didn't say a thing as she was led to her mother's bedside.

When they came in, the doctor stepped out into the hall to give them a moment of privacy.

"Laura?" Jeanette asked groggily when she saw her.

"Yes, it's me. How are you?" she asked in whispered relief. She realized she had been holding her breath.

"I'm all right. I'm just so tired," she said and drifted off to sleep again.

"Will she be all right? What happened to her?" Laura asked the doctor anxiously as soon as they stepped out of the room.

"Tell us the diagnosis," Bill said in a voice full of pain.

"Well, there's no easy way to say this. She suffered a fairly severe stroke. Even with therapy she won't walk again. The chances are she'll be paralyzed on one side of her body the rest of her life," he told them with real regret. "I'm sorry." Then he was gone.

At this news Bill and Laura both started crying. Jeanette had always been so active that it was just so hard to imagine her never even walking again.

Around five o'clock Rob left to take care of some things, but said he'd be back at Laura's house the next morning.

Sometime during those hours that she spent in the hospital room with her Mom, Laura knew that she couldn't be in Rob's movie. She had to go home and take care of her Mom.

Laura took out her cell phone to call Rob, but, discovered that her battery was dead. She went out into the hall and used a payphone.

"Hello."

"Hello, Rob."

"Are you all right? Did something else happen?" he asked in genuine concern.

"No. Mom's resting comfortably."

"How are you coping with all of this, Laura?"

"Not so well, honestly. Mom was always the strong one in the family. I knew I could always count on her and that no matter what she would support me. I'm not going to get any sleep tonight, staying at the hospital, and that definitely doesn't help my emotional state," Laura sighed.

"I can come and pick you up if you want. Come have dinner with me and my family and then I can take you back to your place so you can get some sleep."

"That sounds amazing. Thank you Rob." They agreed that Rob would pick her up at six o'clock.

Laura realized that she still hadn't told him the reason she called. "I have to tell you something Rob, and you aren't going to like it," Laura said miserably.

"Whatever you need to tell me I will understand. All that matters to me right now is to help you get through this time."

"Before I say it, I want you to know that you mean so much to me and that I really hate to say this. So here it goes. Rob, I'm not going to be in your next movie. I'm going to go home and take care of my mom. I'll finish this movie, but I just can't be in the other. I…"

She started to say something, but she was out of time.

That was the way Rob felt at the moment. He had run out of time with Laura Johnson.

"What is it Rob?" Jill asked as she walked into his kitchen and saw the look of pain on his face.

"It was Laura. She's leaving. From the sound of things for good," Rob said pitifully.

Chapter 14

True to his word, Rob was at the hospital right at six. He was still shocked by the news Laura had just given him but he determined that they would just make the best of the time they had left.

"How's your mom?" he asked when Laura got in his car.

"She's doing a little better. The nurse helped her eat almost all of her supper. It's just so hard to see her like this. The doctors just told her before I left."

"How did she take it?"

Laura smiled briefly. "She took it a lot better than Dad, and I did," she admitted the pride for her Mother shining through the pain in her voice.

"So obviously, you need some time off to spend with your family and rightfully, so work is the last thing on your mind right now." Rob turned to Laura to make sure she was paying attention to what he was about to say. "I sent out an email to all the cast and crew. It said that due to circumstances beyond my limited control I'm canceling work on the movie for a week and told them to email me if they had any questions."

"Thank you Rob," she said and leaned over to kiss him on the cheek. "Thank you for canceling."

"You're welcome that way I can be here to support you. Besides, it's the least I could do for the woman I love," Rob said this last part before he made a conscious choice to tell her. It was true though. Every day, he cared about her more than he had the day before. It had snuck up on him, but it was definitely there all the same.

Laura was shocked speechless. She had no idea what to say. She cared for Rob, but she didn't love him.

Rob raked a hand through his hair and thought he had just wrecked their relationship. "Let's just get to my parents' house. We need to talk."

"That sounds good to me," Laura agreed fervently.

They were silent for the rest of the drive. Neither knew exactly what to say.

"How much longer will you be here?"

"I don't know. It depends on when Mom gets released."

"I see."

"Rob?" Laura asked tentatively.

"Yes, Laura?"

"Did you mean what you said?"

"Yes, Laura, I did."

"I see."

Laura was at a loss for words.

Rob knew that Laura was exhausted. So he ended the conversation by saying, "I'm not sorry that I told you Laura, because what I said is true, but I know that was just about the worst time I could have said it. Obviously, there's more to be said, but I don't think that time is now. Would you still want to come over for dinner?"

After thinking about it for a moment, she replied, "I think I'd rather go home and sleep. I got less than three hours last night. Is it cold in here?" Laura asked her teeth starting to chatter.

Rob thought it was too warm in the car, but he still turned on the heat for Laura. "I'll gladly take you home, then you just call me when you're ready to go back."

Laura fell asleep as soon as she let her head rest on the back of the seat. When they got to Laura's house, she was still asleep.

Rob had no idea what to do. He noticed for the first time that she hadn't brought her purse with her. After a few minutes of indecision, he decided to try her door to see if it was unlocked.

It wasn't. Next he searched the porch to see if she had a key outside. There he came up with nothing again. So after thinking it over he decided to take her to his house and, if she wasn't awake he would put her on his couch and let her sleep.

With this thought firmly in mind, he started driving to his house. Once he got home he went and opened the front door. Then he came back to the car opened the passenger door and carried Laura into the house.

Laura slept through the whole thing.

Jill entered the living room as Rob laid Laura on the sofa. She quickly surmised the situation.

"Mind if I take a guess as to what's going on?"

"Sure, go ahead."

"You offered to take Laura to visit her mom but she fell asleep on the way there. You then proceeded to come here in order to let her sleep."

"That's pretty much it. She told me that she only got three hours of sleep last night," he replied in a whisper.

"Was she worried about her mom?"

Rob just nodded.

Chapter 15

She slept the rest of the afternoon. When Laura woke up and looked around at her surroundings, she felt disoriented.

"Where am I?" she asked the room at large.

Just then Rob walked into the room.

"Oh, I'm glad to see you're awake. Did you sleep well?" he asked with a smile.

Laura just frowned and nodded. "Where am I?" she asked again.

Rob's smile faded. "This is my house. Don't you remember? You came to my house for church. Isn't any of this ringing a bell?" he asked in concern.

Laura nodded. "Can I sleep some more?"

"Sure, I hope you sleep well."

She did.

The first time Rob came to check in on her, it was two o'clock. He covered her with an extra blanket when he saw the goose bumps on her arms.

When they were about to sit down to the table for dinner, Laura was still asleep.

He started to worry about her. It was now seven o'clock.

When Rob went to check on Laura, she was sitting up on the couch.

"How are you?"

"Fine, did you try to talk to me earlier?" she asked with a frown.

Rob nodded. "Do you remember it at all, besides that I talked to you?"

Laura thought a minute. "Not really. Your couch is too warm."

"Thanks. Are you hungry?" he asked starting to feel relieved.

"I am. What time is it?" she asked still trying to wake up completely.

"It is," Rob said consulting his watch, "just after seven. Will you eat with us?"

"Sure, do you mind if I use your phone first? I want to call Dad and tell him where I am."

Rob led her to the phone.

Laura decided that her best choice would be to call her dad's cell phone.

He answered on the first ring.

"Hello."

"Hi Dad, I'm sorry that I didn't call you and let you know where I was."

"Laura? Where are you? I've been trying to call your cell phone for the last couple of hours."

"I fell asleep on Rob's couch. I didn't sleep well last night. I went to the studio, but he cancelled the shoot. He offered to take me home, but I fell asleep in his car. So he took me back to his place, where I have been sleeping on his couch for the last several hours."

"I see. That makes sense."

"How's Mom doing?"

"Great. The doctors say that they're going to release her tomorrow. Her blood pressure is still above where they want it but as long as that goes down she's a free woman tomorrow."

"That is good news. I have to go. I'll call you later."

"All right."

And with just a few more words they both hung up the phone.

"I'm glad that you decided to join us Laura," Jill said as Laura made her way into the kitchen.

"Thank you. I'm sorry to have held you up."

"That's all right," they all assured her.

"How's your mom?" Bob asked.

"Better. She's supposed to be coming home tomorrow," Laura said with a smile. She suddenly realized that she hadn't eaten all day. She was glad that they let her serve herself first.

When Rob saw how little Laura took he commented.

"Feel free to take as much as you want. There's plenty more food in the kitchen."

Laura, feeling a little sheepish, took another serving of all the food.

"Thanks."

"You're welcome."

The night progressed much too quickly. It was an evening of celebration. More so when she remembered how well her mom was recovering.

Eventually, it was just Rob and Laura in the room.

"I'm glad that your mom is so much better," he told her honestly.

"I am too. How long do you think that it'll take to finish making the movie?" she asked quietly. She was thinking about how much longer she had with Rob.

"It will likely take a week or two. Have you told your parents what you plan to do?"

"No, not yet. I haven't had a chance. I can't explain why, but I know that I have to go home and take care of my mom. Please tell me that you understand."

"I do. It makes complete sense. The same thing happened when I gave you that job. I didn't know why but I knew that you were supposed to have that job."

"Thanks for understanding Rob."

"You're welcome," he paused then said, "I'm glad that I did. I've loved working with you. Please tell me that we'll stay in touch," he almost pleaded.

"Of course Rob. I would hate it if we didn't write each other," Laura laughed. "Listen to us. We're acting as if I'm going away to the deepest, darkest jungle of Africa, or someplace equally far away," she said and then in a voice so soft Rob almost missed it she whispered," Rob?"

"Yeah?"

"I'm going to miss you."

"I'm going to miss you too. What are you going to do when you go home?" Rob asked changing the subject.

"You mean what will I do to make money?"

Rob nodded.

"Nothing, I'll be too busy helping my Dad with the cooking and cleaning and all of those jobs."

Rob had already thought about the fact that Laura most likely wouldn't get a job, but he was still concerned for her financially. If she's careful with the money, she got when she started; it should take care of her for a while. Then he got the idea to have his church group raise some money for Laura. He would have to work fast and keep it a surprise, but he thought the church would be more than happy to support Laura in this. Finally, he started to relax.

They talked for the next two hours.

They would have talked into the early hours of the morning. However, Rob's parents came in to tell them they were going to bed.

"Goodnight, Rob. We're pretty tired so we'll see you in the morning. I'm glad we had the opportunity to get to know you better Laura."

"It was good to get to know you two also. What time is it?"

"It is 10:45."

"Oh, my goodness; I didn't realize that it was that late. I guess I'd better be getting home myself," Laura said on a yawn.

"I'll go get my coat, and we'll leave," he said as his parents walked from the room.

"You're taking me home? Why are you doing that?" Even as she asked the questions she knew what the answer was. "I forgot that I didn't drive myself."

They left Rob's house shortly after that. Conversation was brief on the way to Laura's rental home.

"Thank you for taking me home Rob."

"You're welcome, Laura. What time do you want me to pick you up tomorrow?"

"How about nine o'clock? Does that work?"

"Nine sounds good to me. I'll see you in the morning," Rob told her, then leaned forward and gave her a gentle kiss on the lips. It was a brief kiss but very nice.

Anything that Laura had been planning to say left her in a rush.

Rob felt the same way. He made himself walk away after telling her a soft goodnight. Something didn't seem right with Laura. He prayed that she would be herself tomorrow when he picked her up to take her back to the hospital.

Chapter 16

At six o'clock, the next morning and Laura was miserable. She hadn't slept at all, and she couldn't get comfortable.

First she was hot. Then she was cold. Her throat felt like it was on fire.

She knew that she was sick. She decided to take her temperature to see if she needed medicine or a doctor. Laura was shocked when the thermometer read 103.5. Then she was unsure of what to do. She tried to think about whom she should call.

At first she thought of calling her dad but didn't want to worry him. Then she thought of calling an ambulance but didn't think that that would be necessary.

Finally, she decided to call Rob.

He answered on the second ring.

"Hello?" Rob answered in a tired voice.

"Rob, I need you to come and take me to the hospital," she told him as the room started to spin. "Rob, hurry! I'm…" she started to say but then passed out.

"Laura? Are you all right?"

When she didn't answer, he rushed to get dressed.

He made it to Laura's house in record time. He had broken every speed limit. Rob tried to wake Laura up, but it didn't work. So he picked her up and carried her to his car.

When they got to the hospital Laura woke up.

She was able to walk, with the help from Rob, into the hospital.

"Hello. What are her symptoms?" the man at the front desk asked.

"My girlfriend called me this morning. She asked me to pick her up so that I could bring her here to visit her mother. Before she finished she passed out."

Moments later Laura was checked into a room.

Rob tried to follow but was detained.

"I need you to fill out this paperwork."

"I don't think I can. I'm not a family member. Her father's here. Just not in this wing. He's visiting his wife," he was babbling. He finished with, "I could take them to him for you." He wanted to be the one to tell Bill what happened.

"I'm sorry. I'm the only one who can take these to him. But, I can't stop you from following me."

Once Rob got to the hospital wing where he knew Jeanette was, he wasn't feeling quite as glad to be the one to tell Bill.

His concern doubled when he got to her room and found it empty. He checked his watch. 7:15. He didn't think that they had released her yet.

He quickly walked to the nurse's station.

"May I help you?"

"Will you please tell me what happened to Jeanette Johnson?"

"I'm sorry. That information is reserved for family only right now."

Rob grew more worried with each step, but continued to follow the nurse to a conference room where he finally found Bill, sitting alone.

"Rob, what are you doing here? How did you know to find me?"

"I followed the nurse," Rob said simply.

Before Rob could say another word, the nurse put the paperwork in front of Bill. The top of the form said ADMISSION. "What is this?"

"Your daughter Laura is being admitted as we speak. She is presenting with a high fever, and her throat is swollen. At this point, we think it may be tonsillitis. I'll send the doctor in to give you more information. Right now, though I need you to fill out this paperwork and sign this paper giving us permission to operate should we need to go in that direction."

Bill signed without thinking about it. He had just lost his wife. He would not lose both people he cared most about in life in the same week.

After getting the forms filled out and turned in Bill finally found his voice. "Rob, what in the world is happening right now? Yesterday, both of the women in my life were fine. Now one's dead, and the other's in the hospital possibly facing surgery?" His voiced cracked on the last word. "Tell me something!"

"Laura called me this morning. She said that she needed to come to the hospital. Then she passed out. I rushed her straight here. What happened to Jeanette?" Rob asked though he knew by now that Jeanette was no longer alive.

How could this happen? Bill kept asking himself. He tried to stand but couldn't. "Her blood pressure kept rising last night. Nothing the doctors did could control it. She had another stroke about six o'clock this morning. She didn't make it."

"I'm so sorry, Bill."

Just then, they heard a knock on the conference room door and the doctor walked in. He introduced himself as Dr. Blake Shelton.

After shaking his hand, Bill asked, "So what can you tell me?"

"Your daughter has a high temperature and a severe case of

tonsillitis. She needs to have a tonsillectomy. As soon as her fever has left, and her vital signs stabilize we'll operate. It's a routine procedure. She's going to be just fine."

"Is she awake?" Bill asked quietly.

The doctor nodded and led them to her room, then stayed outside to give them privacy.

When they entered they could hear her talking. Laura kept on saying one word, Mom.

It was almost more than Bill or even Rob could stand.

"Hi Laura, how are you feeling honey?" Bill asked.

"Not too good. I'm so tired."

"You just go to sleep. Rob, or I, or both of us will be here when you wake up," he told her.

"Is Rob here?"

Rob came close to her bed.

"Thank you," she said very softly.

Rob wasn't given a chance to reply. She was already asleep.

"Thank you for not kicking me out, sir."

"Call me Bill. I know what it's like to see a woman you love in one of these beds," he replied with tears in his eyes.

Chapter 17

Laura slept on and off that day. By that evening, her temperature was back to normal.

She was in and out of surgery by three o'clock, and it looked like she would recover.

She still didn't know about her mother's death.

Bill knew that he had to tell Laura today. He didn't want to, but he decided to tell her the next time that she was awake.

That time came before he was ready. He didn't quite know how to tell her. She took the choice out of his hands.

"Dad, where's Mom? I thought that she was supposed to be released yesterday. Did she come and I just missed her?"

All that Bill could do was shake his head.

"Why wasn't she released?"

"She died yesterday morning. She had another massive stroke."

He watched Laura's monitor closely to make sure she wasn't getting too worked up, though, under the circumstances, it was certainly reasonable. She was still weak from the surgery.

"But you said the doctors told you she was fine as long as her blood pressure stayed normal. Why didn't they monitor her more closely? They should have done something!" Laura croaked.

Bill took Laura's hand in both of his own. "Sweetheart, I know you're upset, you need to calm down right now. The doctors are worried about your heart rate. Try taking some deep breaths."

Not until Bill saw her heart rate returning to normal did he continue. "The doctor's did everything they could. It was just her time to go."

When he finished both were openly sobbing.

Bill and Laura hugged for a long time.

The doctor and nurse came in just as they pulled away.

"I've got some good news Laura," Doctor Shelton told them. "You're going to be released this evening. Right now I just want you to rest and take it easy. Try to eat a couple of ice chips but go pretty easy for now."

"That is good news," Bill said and thanked him.

Fifteen minutes later the doctor and his nurse were leaving.

"Dad, when is the funeral?"

"It's on Thursday."

Laura started crying again and fell asleep.

When she woke up, she saw Rob coming in with a wheelchair.

"Thanks Rob. Why do I have to be in a wheelchair?" she asked, not liking the idea at all.

"The surgery and fever have weakened you. You need to get back your strength," Bill told her in a patient voice.

Laura sighed. "Did the doctor say how long I would need to use it?"

Nobody knew.

"I'll go check. You two go ahead. I'll come and visit you later," offered Rob.

Bill and Laura said little as they went to Bill's car and got Laura situated.

"Dad, I've made a decision," she announced as they left the parking lot. When Bill said nothing Laura continued, "You're probably thinking that I shouldn't make any decisions, right now, but I really decided before I found out about Mom."

"Go ahead and tell me your idea," he told her.

"I'm going to come home and help around the house."

"You'd be willing to give up Hollywood and fame?"

"Of course I am. I'll finish up this movie and then I'm coming home."

"What about Rob?"

"What about him?" she asked feeling hurt.

"You mean you'd be willing to give up Rob?" Bill asked in surprise.

"Dad, I care about Rob. I've enjoyed spending time with him, and I think a lot of him but I don't love him. I can still be his friend. You're my only family. Family needs to stick together."

"You're right Laura. I'm just feeling insignificant. That's all."

"Well, it isn't true."

Bill didn't know what to say, so he didn't say anything.

"Is it possible that I'm tired again?"

Bill smiled compassionately. "Being sick will do that to you."

Laura was soon fast asleep.

It was just after supper when Rob came to visit Laura. He was surprised when Laura answered the door, without her wheelchair.

"Hi Rob. Please come in," she invited.

"Thanks. I came to tell you that you don't need to be in a wheelchair, but I guess that you've already found that out yourself. How are you?"

"Physically or emotionally?" she asked.

"Both."

"Physically I'm all right. I'm still really weak though. Emotionally I don't know. I think that a part of me is still in shock. I mean she was supposed to be released from the hospital. It still doesn't feel real at all."

"I wish that I knew what to say. I can't imagine what it must be like not getting to say good-bye though. I'm praying for you Laura. I wanted you to know that."

"Thank you Rob. How long will it take to finish filming?"

"A week from whenever you start."

After seeing Laura's confused expression he explained, "I've had everyone else doing their parts. So, when you come back to work we'll have you doing your acting, and we'll splice them together."

"I see."

An awkward silence fell. Neither knew what to say.

Rob wished he could give her more encouragement but had no idea what to say.

Laura wished that she wasn't feeling exhausted and like she could cry at the drop of a hat all the time.

"When will I stop being tired?" she asked on a yawn.

Rob smiled tenderly. "You'll probably feel that way for a week. I should go and let you sleep."

"I'm sorry Rob. I wish that I wasn't feeling so tired."

"I understand completely. May I ask one question before I go?"

"Of course, you can."

"Do you know when you'll be able to come back to the studio?"

"I'll come in two days after tomorrow. Does that work at all?"

"Give yourself as much time as you need. Why don't you take at least a week off work? It really wouldn't make that much of a difference."

Laura shook her head. "I just want to finish so I can go home.

Can you understand that?" Laura asked her eyes filling with tears again.

Rob nodded. "Goodnight Laura. I hope you sleep well."

"Thanks Rob. Good night."

Rob left a few seconds later.

Laura went to bed and slept all through the night.

Chapter 18

On the day of the funeral, it finally hit her. She hadn't wanted to accept the facts. Not even acknowledge that something like this could happen. But it had. Her mother was gone. Laura sobbed.

In the midst of her crying her father came in and held her. By the end, Bill was crying too.

"What time do we need to leave for the funeral?" Laura asked a little shakily.

"We should leave in about forty-five minutes."

At that point, both ran out of words. They finished getting ready and left the house without further conversation.

Laura was amazed at how many people came to her mother's funeral. She was especially surprised that they were there on such short notice.

Laura was overwhelmed when her church family came to lend support.

It wasn't an overly long funeral, but nice. The flowers were simple yet elegant.

After the funeral, they held a lunch for those who came. The meal consisted of ham and cheese sandwiches, potato salad and a drink.

Rob and Laura didn't get a chance to say much to each other. He came to visit Laura after a couple hours, to give Bill and Laura some privacy.

Laura answered the door on the second knock.

"Hi."

Laura was still in the dress that Rob had seen her in at the funeral.

"I'm sorry she's gone," he told her softly.

"Come on in Rob"

They moved into the living room to talk. Laura took the chair, and Rob took the sofa next to her.

"I'm coming into the studio to work tomorrow," she informed Rob after several minutes of silence.

"Are you sure that you're up to it?" Rob asked.

Laura nodded. "I'm ready to be getting home."

"I can understand that."

Rob could tell that Laura was exhausted and suggested she take a nap.

"I think I will. I'm sorry."

"Why are you sorry?"

"I haven't been good company. All I do is sleep and cry."

"I understand Laura."

"Thanks."

Rob left a few minutes later.

The last days of filming were less than pleasant.

Laura was excited about going home, but knew she would miss Rob.

Rob, noticing Laura's happiness and eagerness to go home was filled with dread.

It was the last day of filming, and Rob was feeling even more miserable than before.

Both were silent when Laura completed her final scene.

"Laura?" Rob called to her when it looked like she would leave.

"Yes?"

"Will you have dinner with me one last time before you go?"

"I can't. I have to finish packing."

"Oh. Okay. Well, I'm sure you have a lot of that to do; so, I'll just let you go."

"Rob?" Laura said quickly afraid he would just walk away.

"Yes, Laura?"

"Can we make it a quick lunch instead of dinner?" she asked not wanting their relationship to end on such a sad note.

The two were silent as they made their way to Claire's.

"Are you all right Laura?"

"Listen Rob, I know you're trying to be sweet but, right now, asking me if I'm okay is kind of an inappropriate question."

Rob dropped his eyes. "You're right. I shouldn't have asked you that. You're leaving tomorrow aren't you?" he asked changing the subject.

Laura nodded. "We're going to try to leave by seven."

Their food arrived minutes later.

"Laura can I have your address and phone number?"

"You want my address in Dallas?"

Rob nodded.

"Why would you want that?"

Rob looked hurt but still answered. "I told you I wanted to keep in touch. Did you think I lied to you?"

"I don't know. It just never happens."

"What never happens?"

"Long distance relationships. People always say they'll keep in touch but don't."

"Laura if you think that I'm just suddenly going to stop caring about you you're wrong."

"I'm sorry Rob. I really don't know what else to say."

"The decision is yours, Laura. I promise I'll write as many letters to you as you write to me."

"Thanks Rob."

They talked for a few more minutes, but then Laura said she had to go and finish packing.

"Will you call me tonight and tell me for sure when you're leaving?"

"Sure, thank you for lunch Rob."

"It was my pleasure. I'll see you tomorrow."

Seconds later they both left the restaurant.

"Hi Dad," Laura said on a sigh as she walked in the door.

"Hi Laura, how was your day?" he asked in a teary voice.

"It was all right I guess. I'm glad we're leaving tomorrow."

"I'm anxious to go home too."

"When do you want to leave in the morning?"

"I'm hoping to leave by eight. Does that work for you?"

Bill nodded.

"How was your day Dad?" Laura asked.

"Lonely," he told her honestly.

"It's hard isn't it? It still doesn't seem like she's gone." Instead of crying in front of her dad, she went to her room to take a nap.

When Laura woke up, Rob was on her mind. She started to think about life in Dallas and already started to miss Rob.

This is ridiculous. She thought to herself. *I haven't even left, and I miss him.*

She tried to tell herself not to call, but it didn't work for long.

So she gave up and dialed the now memorized number.

"Hi Rob. You're home later than you thought you would be aren't you?" Jill asked looking at the clock.

"Yeah, I talked to Laura. She and I had lunch together."

"How did that go?" she asked wondering about the tone in his voice.

"I don't know. I'm not sure how I feel about how it ended. What do you want me to fix for supper?" Rob sighed.

"Well, I haven't had…" she began but was interrupted when the phone rang.

"Hello?"

There was a period of silence. Rob was about to hang up when Laura's soft voice came over the line.

"Hi, Rob."

"Hi Laura, how are you?"

"I'm all right. Dad and I are leaving at eight tomorrow," she told him upfront.

"Oh." He said inanely. "Do you want me to come and help with packing the moving van?"

"No thank you. I'm sorry Rob, but I really need to go."

"Okay. Thanks for calling."

"Bye."

With that she hung up the phone.

"Laura?" Jill asked needlessly.

Rob nodded.

They didn't say another word about it as Rob started to make spaghetti.

That night Laura slept fitfully. She kept thinking about her mom, and about having to go back home to all the memories.

She thought of all the times helping her mom in the kitchen when she was younger and the wonderful times the two of them had baking chocolate chip cookies. Then there were the memories of sewing with her mom. The first pair of pants they had sewed together.

Laura hadn't wanted to but, at the end of her collage of memories she started crying.

Laura glanced at the digital clock next to her bed. It was 1:30. She sighed. If this keeps up it'll be a long night. She thought to herself.

She closed her eyes thinking to at least rest. When she opened her eyes light streamed through her windows and her alarm was about to go off.

She didn't get up right away but prayed about the day and the ones to come. After finishing, she felt a peace she hadn't known in too long.

Rob woke up early the next morning. He wanted to say good-bye to Laura before she left. After debating with himself, he decided to drop by her apartment at seven thirty.

Chapter 19

Rob pulled up to Laura's house at 7:35. He got out of his car and slowly walked up her driveway.

"Hi Rob," Laura said softly. She wasn't looking forward to this at all.

"Hi."

"Thanks for coming."

"You're welcome."

"I'm going to miss you Rob. You've been my best friend. I'm sorry, but at this point I can't handle anything more than friendship."

"I'm going to miss you too. I respect your decision of friendship, but I can't let you go without telling you one thing. I love you and always will."

Rob saw her mouth open, but no sound was made. A large lump formed in Rob's throat. He realized that Laura didn't love him.

"Maybe, in another time and another place I could say the same but, if I said it now it would just be my grief talking and you deserve more than that. I'm going to miss you too. You gave me a job when I thought my only option was to go back home." Laura gave him a mighty hug then asked, "I gave you my address and phone number didn't I?"

"Yes you did. What day will you get to Dallas?"

"I think we'll get there some time Friday afternoon."

"That'll be a long drive." Rob stated the obvious.

Laura glanced down at her watch and groaned. It was 7:55.

Rob knew he was almost out of time.

"I have to go soon," Laura said unnecessarily.

"I wish you didn't have to leave; but I understand. Good-bye Laura. Have a safe trip," Rob told her giving her one last hug.

"Good-bye Rob," Laura told him barely keeping her tears at bay.

Laura thought that it would be a long trip, and she was right.

They planned to make the trip in two days, and they were at the end of their first day.

Bill's uncle Roger, who lived in Arizona, had invited Laura and Bill to stay with them for the night. They gratefully accepted.

The next morning they were served a large breakfast and given a lunch for the road.

Even though Laura was grateful to her uncle she was anxious for her own bed.

Bill and Laura talked on and off, but the majority of the trip was made in silence. An hour into their trip the second day Bill asked Laura what she would be doing when they got home.

"I'll be helping you around the house. Why do you ask?" Laura asked in confusion.

"I just wondered if you would be getting a job."

"I haven't thought about it. Why?" she asked again.

"I've decided to retire. Maybe sell the house."

"What are you talking about? Why would you sell the house?"

"I've been thinking about it for a while. Even before your mom died, I wanted to move out into the country. I'm tired of the hustle and bustle.

Laura could understand that. Her dad was raised on a farm. The closest large town was forty-five minutes away.

Finally she asked, "Where would you move?"

"I'm not sure. I thought one of the Midwestern states."

"I see."

With that nothing, more was said about Bill moving or retiring.

Since Bill still felt wide-awake Laura slept once again. While Laura slept, Bill thought about the last several days and all the many things that had transpired.

In one and a half weeks his wife died, and his only child had been taken to the hospital and had to have surgery.

Bill's only thought as he continued down the road was, I hope that life goes back to some level of normalcy again.

Around the time that Bill and Laura were arriving at their Dallas home, Rob started to miss Laura tremendously.

Yesterday Rob hadn't let himself think of Laura. He distracted himself by showing his parents the sights. Again. It wasn't affective, but it helped a little bit.

Now he had just left the airport from seeing his parents off at the airport. Now what was he going to do?

At ten, minutes until six o'clock Laura drove into their garage.

In Laura's eyes, nothing could have looked better. She couldn't wait to crawl into her own bed. Although she was glad to be home, she knew it would bring a measure of sadness.

Some moments it still didn't feel real.

"It sure is good to be home," Bill said softly remembering when he and Jeanette bought this house.

"Well, I guess we should unpack," Laura said knowing it was a lame statement.

Five minutes into unloading the van a red four door '95 Corsica pulled into the driveway.

Laura didn't immediately recognize the man that got out of the car. She finally recognized him to be Andy Copeland. He hadn't been around for the past couple years because he was away at college.

He seemed taller than the last time that Laura had seen him. And, even though she thought it would have been impossible, he looked even better than he did in high school. She hadn't seen him in close to three years, but one look was enough to make her heart start pounding again. *Get a grip on yourself Laura Johnson. You can't trust your emotions right now. Besides, don't forget how mean he was to you in high school. Be friendly and courteous but that's it.*

"Hello Laura," he greeted her, his voice a rich baritone.

"Hi. How are you?"

"I'm pretty good. How are you?" he asked, suddenly feeling shy, which was a new experience for him. "I was sorry to hear about your mom," he said after a moment.

"Thanks."

"I came to ask you and Bill to come to dinner tonight. I figured that you wouldn't want to cook," he said in the way of explanation.

"Let me go check."

She came back a short time later.

"We'll be happy to come. When do you want us?" she asked relieved not to have to cook.

"How much time do you need?" he asked kindly.

"Would fifteen to twenty minutes from now work okay?"

"That sounds good to me."

Chapter 20

Fifteen minutes later Bill and Laura arrived at Andy Copeland's Tudor-style house.

Their knock was answered quickly.

"Hi," Andy greeted them warmly. "Please come in."

"Thank you."

Andy led them both to a very comfortable yet elegant looking living room. There were many paintings on the wall and vases of fresh flowers graced one end table.

"Please make yourselves comfortable."

"Can I do anything to help with dinner?" Laura asked even though she had started to sit down on the couch. She thought she would have been tired of sitting after all the driving they had done but she still felt weary.

"No, just sit down and rest. Dinner will be ready soon."

Laura took the time to look around the room. Matching sofas were turned at an angle conducive to conversation.

The centerpiece of the room was a large fireplace and mantle.

The floor was hardwood with an elegant rug.

Just as Laura finished looking around at the beautiful furnishings Andy came back in the room to tell them that supper was ready.

The dining room was a fairly large room with a round table that looked like it would seat five comfortably.

"Please sit down."

"Everything looks great," Laura told him honestly.

And it did. Andy had fixed pork chops, mashed potatoes and broccoli with cheese.

"Thank you."

After Andy had prayed for the meal, they began to eat.

"These pork chops are really good. What seasoning did you put on it?" she asked thinking that Andy hadn't changed much over the years.

"It's a family secret," he told her with a grin.

The night was filled with good conversation and good food. After the main course, they had chocolate cake and chocolate ice cream.

By eight, thirty Bill looked like he could fall asleep in his chair.

Laura realized how tired she was, as well. They thanked Andy for a wonderful night and left.

Laura felt anxious about the next day. She knew that she would have to clean the house and do all of the things that her mother had done.

She fell asleep five minutes after getting into the car.

Bill didn't want Laura to wake up so he carried her into the house and tucked her in bed. Shortly after putting Laura to bed Bill readied himself for bed.

They both slept until noon the next day.

Laura stretched, yawned, and got out of bed.

She walked out to the kitchen and found her dad sitting at the table.

"Morning Dad," Laura greeted with a yawn.

"Good morning,"

"What time did you get up?"

"It was around eleven thirty," he speculated.

Laura nodded, and opened the door of the refrigerator but turned back to ask, "So is the memorial service tomorrow?"

Bill nodded, and tears once more came to his eyes.

In order to give her Dad some privacy, she turned her attention back to the fridge thinking about what she could cook for dinner. What she saw made her jaw drop. The fridge was absolutely full of food. There were salads and meats and vegetables and casseroles not to mention all the desserts that people had brought.

She heard God's voice telling her; *I love you. I'm going to provide for you. You are my beloved child. And then a verse came to mind. It had been one of the verses she memorized as a child. Psalms 34:18: The Lord is near to the brokenhearted and saves the crushed in spirit.*

Hearing this Laura broke down in the middle of the kitchen. "What…? Who…? When did…?" she stammered not able to say anything.

"I haven't got a clue. This is the first I've seen it," Bill replied just as flabbergasted as Laura was.

"I don't quite know what to do or say," she exclaimed. She stopped to pray and thank God for providing for them.

"I don't know what to say either."

Both were speechless and sat completely still for five minutes before Laura got back up and heated some food for her dad and herself. *Just keep moving.* She told herself. *If you keep moving you'll be fine.*

As Laura heated a plate of food someone came to the door and knocked.

"I'll get that," Bill told her.

Laura heard him answer but couldn't tell who was there.

She soon found out as Andy followed her dad into the kitchen.

"Hi, Laura."

"Hello Andy. How are you?" That familiar knot of nerves was back in Laura's stomach. She hated that he could still do this to her after so many years.

"I'm doing all right."

Bill excused himself and left the two alone.

"Would you like to sit down?" Laura asked.

Andy gratefully took a seat, and a short time later, plate in hand, Laura joined him. They talked about the memorial service that was to be held the next day, and he soon left to let her get some rest.

With everything that had happened in the last month sleep was the only thing that came easily to Laura.

The next morning dawned bright and clear, not a cloud in sight. All it did was make Laura angry. It should have been pouring down rain. It wasn't fair that they had to do this again. They had a funeral for her in California. Why did they have to go through all of this again? Laura tired of the sympathy. All the sympathy in the world wouldn't change the fact that she would never see her mom on this earth again.

She sighed heavily and decided that maybe this memorial was really more for the people here than for her and Dad. After all, half of Jeanette's closest friends hadn't been able to attend the first service.

By the end of the day her attitude had improved somewhat and she was able to appreciate what people said to her. She found it especially thoughtful when people would give her pictures of their favorite memories of Jeanette.

Andy sought Laura out to express his condolences; but it was no easy task to find a time when she was alone. "Thank you for helping with the service Andy. I really appreciated the kind words you had to say."

"Oh, it was my pleasure. I know everyone has told you this, but your mother was one of the kindest women I knew. I'm sure this isn't the best timing, but if you ever need a friend or someone to help you process things, I want to be here to help," he told her unsure of himself. "It doesn't have to be anything as formal as coming by the church office or anything. We could just go grab a coffee. Whatever you're most comfortable with," he ended feeling his cheeks grow red.

"I may take you up on that sometime."

The two talked of general things until Andy's cell phone beeped telling him he had a voicemail.

"Do you need to call someone?" Laura asked after he consulted it.

"I'm afraid I have to go. Why don't you call me whenever you feel up for it?"

"That sounds good to me."

"Great. I'll be praying for you and Bill," and then he excused himself to listen to the message on his phone.

Laura couldn't help but feel miffed when a few minutes later she saw him walk out of the church. *I guess some things never do change. I was never a priority back then, and I'm not a priority now. Maybe I should just forget about the coffee.*

Chapter 21

Later that afternoon,Laura,got an unexpected call.

"Hello."

"Hi Laura."

"Oh! Hi, Rob. How are you?" Laura asked in surprise.

"I'm doing pretty well. How about you?" he asked in return.

"I'm okay. I'm feeling overwhelmed at the moment."

"Why is that?" Rob asked quietly.

"We got a tremendous amount of food from friends and our church family," she said in explanation.

"That was nice of them."

Soon after this they ran out of things to say.

"I guess I'll let you go now," Rob said reluctantly.

"Wait."

"What?"

"Did you call for a particular reason?"

"No, not really, I just wanted to say hi and that I love you."

"That was kind of you," Laura said with a smile.

"I know," he replied jokingly.

They hung up a short time later.

The next day Laura got up at eight o'clock, had breakfast, and did a load of laundry.

She wondered how long she would feel this lonely. She remembered what Andy had said at the end of the memorial service and thought that the offer of friendship sounded perfect right now. He hadn't had a chance to prove whether or not he had changed since high school.

Who knows? That phone call that he took at the end of the memorial service could have been an emergency. Don't judge too swiftly. With that pep talk and bit of justification over, she picked up the phone and called Andy.

He quickly agreed to pick her up at one o'clock and arrived right on time.

"Right on the dot. You're very punctual," Laura said, standing on the porch.

"Thanks. I'm not late very often. Have you had lunch?"

"I did, about half an hour before. What about you?" They were walking towards Andy's car now.

"I haven't actually. I had a busy day today."

"Oh."

"Would you mind if I got something to eat? I know that originally the deal was coffee," he said as they pulled out of the driveway.

"Oh. That's fine."

"Thank you."

"Where did you want to eat?"

"I thought we could just do fast food."

"That sounds okay to me."

They were quiet until Andy pulled into the parking lot of Burger King.

"What are you hungry for?" Laura asked.

"I'm feeling pretty classic today; I think I'll get a cheeseburger and French fries. What do you want?"

"Well, it's about as far away from coffee as you can get but I think a strawberry milk shake sounds wonderful," she decided on the spot.

"Then a strawberry milk shake you shall have," he told her with a smile.

Laura didn't even wait until they found a seat before she took a long swallow from her milk shake. "This is absolutely delicious."

"I'm glad you like it."

After a pause, Andy asked, "So, what was it like to be in Hollywood?"

"Do you want the long version or the short version?"

After thinking for a moment he said, "I guess the short version."

For just a moment, Laura looked disappointed, and it made Andy wish he had asked for the longer version of her story.

"There was definitely no chance of getting bored out there. There were people everywhere. There was a large selection of restaurants too."

"That's cool. I guess I should have asked you to tell me what happened while you were there."

"Let's see… where to begin. When I got to Hollywood, I went to the studio where I was to audition. It turns out they had given the job to somebody else. So to make a long story short I found another job because I sat at the right lunch table. Rob, the man who gave me the job, asked me to go out with him soon after I started. We started going out a lot, so I asked him to meet my parents before we went much further. He agreed and then things just progressed from there."

"Sounds like you had quite the adventure." Andy said when she finished her story.

"It was. So, how have things been going for you?" she asked getting conversation off of herself.

"It's been going okay; nothing as exciting what you've been telling me. Two months ago I graduated from seminary, and I'm a pastor at the church where we grew up."

"Congratulations. I didn't realize how long it's been since we talked. Has the church changed at all?" she asked excitedly.

"It's going great. The church is growing steadily. God has really shown Himself in fresh ways."

"That's excellent. I'll come on Sunday."

"I look forward to it. I have to ask. How are you doing without your mom?"

"I'm better some days than others. I miss her a lot," she said with tears in her eyes. "It just doesn't seem fair. I'm sure that sounds childish."

"Not at all. God understands our pain and anger when someone we love is taken away from us. Don't forget, He lost His Son, too."

Laura sniffed and wiped her eyes on a napkin. Andy wished he had a handkerchief to offer her. He decided then to get one for such times as this.

There was a long pause before Andy asked, "Do you miss being in Hollywood?" He felt like she needed to be rescued.

"Hmm…" she said grateful for the distraction, "I do in some ways and not in others."

"Did you meet any stars?"

"You mean famous actors? No, just a lot of people like me."

"I think you're a great actress," he told her sincerely.

Laura laughed. "How can you say that? You've never even seen me act."

"Yes I have. Don't tell me you don't remember those plays in school."

"I almost forgot."

"Can I have your autograph?"

"Why in the world would you want my autograph?" Laura asked incredulously. There was no in between with him he had ignored her in high school and now all of a sudden he wanted her autograph. What game was he playing?

"I want it so that I one day I can say, I knew Laura Johnson. The two of us grew up together. One day at lunch she gave me her signature. It was a proud day," he said dramatically.

"Come on Andy. Things like that don't happen to me."

Andy mentally cringed. Why did people expect bad things to happen to them?

"I think that's another subject for another time," he told her.

Not much later Andy took Laura back to her house.

"Thanks for the milk shake Andy."

"You're welcome."

Laura was silent for a moment before she said, "I wanted to talk to you about something; but a fast food place isn't appropriate."

"Okay. Do you want to talk about it right now? I have plenty of time before my next appointment."

She shook her head. "Could you come over after dinner tonight?"

"That should be fine. Can you give me some idea about what's on your mind? Does it have to do with your Mom?"

"No, it's nothing like that. You said something today that I wanted you to go into more detail about what you meant."

Andy relaxed, still curious but confident that he hadn't said anything that could have gotten him in trouble. The idea that Laura might be upset with him bothered him more than he cared to think about right now. “In that case, I would be more than happy to come over tonight. What time should I come?”

They agreed on eight, and Andy left moments later.

Laura knew she had been slightly misleading about the nature of what she wanted to talk about; but it was time to get some answers about high school.

Chapter 22

Andy got up to start washing his dinner dishes when the house phone rang. "Hello."

"Hi, Pastor Andy, this is Alice Smith."

"Oh. Hi. What can I do for you?" he asked kindly hearing the tremor in her voice.

"My husband, Jim, just got in a car accident half an hour ago. Can you come and be with us? The doctors are still doing tests," she said in a rush.

After getting the room information from her, he left everything and got in his car. His evening discussion with Laura, completely forgotten.

"Thanks for coming, Pastor."

"You're welcome. What have the doctors said?"

"They said right now it looks like he'll recover, but they don't know the extent of the damage that was done. I know that there's never a good time for something like this to happen, but this is a bad time for extra hospital bills."

"Does Jim's work not give him good benefits?"

"No, they do. I'm pregnant. I had my first ultrasound today. Jim was on his way there from the office when somebody ran a red light."

"Well, Congratulations! Let's pray for all three of you then."

Alice actually smiled then, "Actually, pray for all four of us. It's twins."

Andy prayed quietly, "Lord, thank you for the gift of new life in Alice. Protect her and the babies and please comfort her, and wrap your arms around her, and be with Jim and protect him. Help them to trust you not only for Jim's healing but also, for their finances. Please, give the doctors wisdom in knowing how to help him best. Amen."

"Thank you."

The doctor, who was in charge of Jim's care, came to give Alice an update on him.

"How is he doctor?"

"He's doing well. He's awake and asking for you. I'm going to have to ask you to keep it short though. He's been through quite an ordeal."

"Thanks doctor."

Alice quietly went into her husband's room.

"Hi, Jim," she said just above a whisper.

"Hi," he said his voice as soft as hers.

"How are you?"

"I'm exhausted. How did your doctor visit go?" he asked remembering.

"The babies and I are perfectly healthy," Alice reported fairly beaming.

"How many babies?" He asked his eyes growing huge. After Alice had told him they were going to have twins, he told her, "It's a good thing I'm in this hospital bed."

"Why on earth is that?"

"I would have fainted dead away if I had been at that appointment."

They spent the next half hour marveling about how good God was, and how excited they were to be starting their family.

"How was he?" Andy asked when Alice came back to the waiting room.

"He's tired. But, he was excited about the ultrasound."

"That's excellent. How long does he need to stay?"

"I haven't heard; hopefully, only two or three days. It seems like the pain medication has been helping him. They have his leg in a harness so that his leg can heal better."

There didn't seem to be anything left to say for the next fifteen minutes.

Andy continued to pray as they waited for the results.

Alice just sat in a chair looking at nothing in particular. Her thoughts were interrupted when the doctor came to talk to her again.

"How is he doctor?" Alice asked, coming to her feet.

"He has a broken leg, and a couple of broken ribs but everything considered; he's doing just fine."

Soon after the doctor left, Andy went home, after telling Alice to call him if she needed anything else.

"Thanks again."

"You're welcome."

By the time, Andy got home it was 9:30.

Chapter 23

When Laura got home after her time with Andy, she wished that she would have just said everything she wanted to say right then. Now she had to wait in suspense all afternoon and evening. In order to distract herself from both her grief and her conflicted feelings about Andy, she again worked on cleaning the house.

She felt as though she had to keep working in order to survive her grief. At the same time, she knew that the approach wasn't healthy.

Later she decided to write to Rob. Another distraction. She thought about just taking it to the mailbox but wanted to get out of the house. So, after telling dad her plans she went to the post office.

On her way home, she realized she needed to get a couple of things at the grocery store for dinner. She had to make a sharp turn into the driveway because she had almost passed it before remembering where she was going.

Laura was glad to make an unexpected stop when she spotted one of her church friends, Ami, whom she hadn't connected with since she had gotten back. "Hi Ami."

"Hi Laura! It's great to have you back. I heard about your mom; I'm sorry."

"Thank you."

"How are you doing?"

"I don't really know," she said with tears coming to her eyes.

After a pause Ami asked, "Would you like to come to a Bible study at my house? I'm sure that it would help to have the fellowship."

"That sounds wonderful. When do you meet?"

"Wednesdays at nine thirty. It usually lasts about forty-five minutes."

The conversation ended shortly after that with Laura telling Ami she would see her on Wednesday.

Laura got the items on her list and went home.

Once she started dinner preparations time seemed to disappear. Her heart started beating quicker at ten minutes of eight. At ten after she got a sinking feeling in the pit of her stomach. *He's just running late.* She told herself. At 8:45, she started reading a book and knew that she had been stood up again.

The whole thing reminded Laura of her sixteenth birthday party.

The next day she sort of moped around at home feeling sorry for herself and furious at Andy. He hadn't even called to apologize. So much for punctual.

On Wednesday, her mood improved greatly when she went to the Bible study at Ami's house.

They were doing a study on the characteristics of God. This week the topic was God's love.

Laura learned a lot from the study. Afterwards, she stayed and had coffee and cookies with Ami. "These chocolate chip cookies are delicious," Laura told Ami as people started to leave.

"Thank you."

"You're welcome."

After catching up for an hour, Laura said she had to get home.

"Well, it was great to see you again, Laura. May I give you one piece of advice before you go?"

Laura nodded.

"Make sure you let yourself grieve. You may think you won't be able to survive, but you will."

"I mean no offense but how would you know?"

Ami looked at her watch deciding if she had time to explain. "I have a doctor's appointment to go to soon. Can I tell you more about this next week?"

Laura nodded in understanding. "Sure. I'll see you next week then. Thank you for inviting me."

"You're welcome."

"How was your Bible study?" Bill asked when Laura came home.

"It was good. How was your morning?" she asked going to sit down on the couch.

"It was okay."

"I feel like I could sleep for a week," Laura said tiredly.

"I know what you mean," Bill agreed.

"I feel like I should be doing something though."

Bill just nodded his head in agreement, wondering just how long he would feel like the world was passing him by. He wanted to get out and connect with his church friends again, but all he could do was sit, read, and sleep.

Chapter 24

On Sunday morning, Bill and Laura slept in and went to the eleven o'clock church service. The people who hadn't been able to make it to the funeral came and talked to Bill and Laura.

Everyone came up and told them how sorry, they were for their loss. She knew they meant well; but Laura felt drained after hearing the same question and replying in the same way. It didn't feel genuine, and yet, what else were they supposed to say?

Laura struggled to keep her focus on God but, once she did, the rest of the service was excellent. The worship time was great. When it was time for announcements Bill got up and formally thanked the church for their support.

Then it was time for Andy to give the message. Laura found herself feeling anxious to hear what he had to say.

Father, fill me with your love, and Lord, give me the words that You want me to speak, Andy prayed silently.

Aloud he said, "This morning I'd like us to look at Psalm chapter two. We'll be starting at verse 7 and read to the end of the chapter. You're welcome to follow along, but this morning I would like to read from the Message.

Verse 7: God said, 'You're my son, and today is your birthday. What do you want? Name it: Nations as a present? Continents as a prize? You can command them to dance for you, or throw them out with tomorrow's trash. So rebel-kings use your heads; up-start judges learn your lesson: worship God in adoring embrace, celebrate in trembling awe. Kiss Messiah! Your very lives are in danger; you know; His anger is about to explode but if you make a run for God- you won't regret it!'

"Wow! Aren't these verses powerful? I read those verses and couldn't get them out of my mind. I noticed several things.

"The first thing I want to look at is in verse seven. 'You're my son.' Isn't that awesome? He wants to be our Father. Some of you might be thinking, 'But, Pastor Andy, you don't know what kind of man my father was.' You're right. I don't know, and I don't need to know. God already does. He's not like your earthly father. Your heavenly Father can't make a single mistake. If you go through a difficult time, He's right there draping His arms around you. He's how you get through those rough seasons in life."

He paused to take a drink of water then continued.

"Now look at the next couple of verses. 'And today is your birthday. What do you want? Name it.' Let's stop there for a minute. "In that verse, God tells us that He wants to give us the desires of our hearts. Now does that mean that I'll get everything that I want? I don't think so.

"God isn't a genie that we can tell what we want. It just doesn't work that way. He does, however, give us what is in accordance with His will.

"Finally look at the last verse of chapter two. '...but if you make a run for God- you won't regret it!' I grew up thinking God was distant.

"Recently He's been showing me differently. Why would a distant God send His Son to die for our sins? If He were distant, He wouldn't have made it that way. Only a loving and personal God would do it the way He did.

"John 3:16 says that God so loved the world He gave us His one and only Son.

Let's pray. Father make it clear to us that You want a personal relationship with each one of us in this room. Let's take a moment to pray before I continue the message. Make Your love known today, Father. Not just the head knowledge but make it heart experience. In Jesus name amen."

Laura tried to pay attention to the rest of the sermon; but she couldn't get her mind off of what he had just said. He was so different from the boy she remembered.

After the benediction, Laura went to the back of the sanctuary to talk to Andy.

"That was a good message."

"Thank you. If you ever have questions, feel free to ask."

Laura nodded. "I will."

Bill followed soon after her. "Are you ready to go home?"

Laura nodded again.

They headed home with little conversation.

Chapter 25

On Tuesday when Laura went to get the mail she found a letter from Rob. She decided to wait to open it until she had more time to read it. She had a lot of errands to do, and she knew she wouldn't be able to concentrate on what she read until she finished what she needed to do.

Laura's day was so busy that she didn't remember the letter until after she had cleaned up the supper dishes.

Dear Laura,

How are you? I miss you. Things are really slow here. I haven't quite known what to do with myself. I'll be glad to get back to work.

Enough about me. How are you doing being at home without your mom? I can't imagine how hard that must be for you. Know that I'm praying for you, and thinking of you often.

Love, Rob

Laura, read the letter a second time. She thought that it was sweet of Rob to write mainly to say he missed her. That evening she wrote a letter of her own.

Dear Rob,

I was glad to hear from you. I know I said that I would not be able to be in the next movie but is it too late to change my mind? I think the acting bug bit me worse than I had originally thought. Right now it looks like my dad will be moving into a smaller house, and he will be able to take care of things. Besides, I think I need to be doing something. I guess I like the idea of a distraction. Thanks for praying.

Your friend,
Laura

The next morning, Laura, got a call from Ami.

"Hello."

"Hi, Laura. How are you?" Ami asked.

"I'm all right."

"Would you have lunch with me today or tomorrow?"

"Sure that would work. What time?"

"How about twelve thirty? Does that work?"

"It should. Where do you want to have lunch?"

"I thought I would like to have it at my house. Is that okay with you?" she asked.

"That sounds good to me."

"Do you remember how to get there?" Ami asked, making sure.

"I do."

"All right. See you soon."

Laura looked at her gold watch and was shocked to see that it was already 11:45.

She left twenty-five minutes later, giving herself plenty of time to get there.

"Thanks for coming over on such short notice," Ami greeted Laura.

"It was no trouble," she told her honestly.

Laura took a few minutes to let her eyes wander around the kitchen.

The walls were decorated in a soft yellow with a darker shade sponged on top of it. The cabinets were painted in a complimentary shade of pastel blue.

"You have a lovely kitchen."

"Thank you."

Ami served the chicken salad sandwiches and potato salad just minutes later.

After she prayed and blessed the food, they began to eat.

"This tastes wonderful," Laura told her enthusiastically.

"Thank you."

Laura saw Ami's expression and explained that she hadn't had a sandwich in a long time.

"With all the casseroles we've gotten from people, we've been eating those."

"I see."

Lunch was filled with good fellowship.

After lunch, the two women enjoyed a glass of pink lemonade.

"So, how are you really doing?" Ami asked emphasizing the word really.

"I'm all right. I've been keeping myself busy," Laura admitted.

"I remember when my mom died," Ami said quietly.

"Your mom died? How long ago?"

"She died when I was in the seventh grade."

Before Laura could make a reply Ami continued.

"I remember how busy I made myself. I didn't think I could bear the pain of losing her."

Laura wasn't sure what to say, but Ami spared her from saying anything.

"Take my advice. Let yourself grieve. Don't let it bottled up inside of you."

Right then Laura made herself a promise that she wouldn't be so busy that she didn't grieve.

Not a whole lot later Laura left to go home.

Chapter 26

Hollywood

"How are you Rob?" Sam, Rob's second in command, asked one afternoon.

The two were having lunch together.

"I'm all right. Why do you ask?"

"You don't seem like yourself."

Rob nodded in agreement. Sam was right. He wasn't the same. He hadn't been for about a month.

"Care to share what's on your mind?"

Rob debated about whether he wanted to say anything or not. He usually didn't like to talk about himself with coworkers.

"Do you mind if I guess?" he asked.

"I guess not. What do you think might be causing my distraction, recently?" Rob asked with a small shake of his head and a laugh.

"Would it perhaps concern something that happened this summer?"

Rob nodded.

"Does it have something to do with a former actor maybe?"

Rob smiled sheepishly and nodded once more.

"I thought as much. Would this former actor be Laura Johnson?" Sam asked mischievously.

"Yes, it would," Rob said bashfully.

Sam chuckled.

"What's so funny about that?" Rob asked.

"Nothing. It's just the way that you said it. You sound like you're embarrassed about it."

"I don't know."

"Did she ever make a final decision about coming back or not?" Sam asked Rob. "I know that when she left she said she wouldn't be back. Has she changed her mind?"

This time Rob's smile was genuine. "I just received a letter from her saying that she did change her mind." Rob looked pensive again, "I just don't know where the two of us stand. I still want to date her, but I just don't know if she feels the same way anymore."

Sam let the subject drop.

Rob knew he had some thinking to do when he got home.

DALLAS

It was a few weeks after Laura's lunch with Ami.

She checked the mail and found a thick manila envelope.

Laura was curious, because there was no return address. She opened it as soon as she went in the house. Inside the envelope was a letter from Rob and what appeared to be a manuscript.

Realization dawned. It was the script for her next movie.

She read the letter first.

Dear Laura,

How are you? Did I tell you when this movie would be made? In case I didn't we're looking to start the fifth of January.

Things have started to pick up around here. I can't wait until you get here so we can talk at length. I wish that I didn't have to but I need to go now.

I love you Laura.

Love,
Rob

Laura, re-read the letter and then looked over the script. It was a humorous detective story.

Laura's character was a sidekick to the detective.

She decided to call Rob instead of writing to him.

Rob answered on the second ring.

"Hello."

"Hi Rob."

"Hi Laura, how are you?" Rob asked in surprise.

"I'm doing okay. I just got your letter and my script," Laura told him thinking it was wonderful to talk to him.

"Ah… what do you think of it?"

"It sounds like fun. Are you the detective?" Laura asked hoping that he was.

"I am," Rob replied.

"That's cool."

"Laura?"

"Yes?"

"Can I call you back later on today? I have a meeting that I need to go to," he explained.

"Sure, I understand."

"Thanks. I miss you, Laura," Rob told her sincerely.

"I miss you too, Rob."

They hung up seconds later.

The conversation lingered in both of their minds. Rob thought about how much he loved Laura.

Laura, on the other hand, thought about how much she was going to miss her new friend Andy when she left. *I know things aren't perfect between us, and I still need answers about high school; but it doesn't change how I feel about him,* she admitted to herself.

In Hollywood Rob mentally went over how long the meeting would be until he could call Laura back.

Laura eagerly awaited Rob's call.

She spent the time reading her Bible and praying.

At four o'clock, Laura's time, the call she had been waiting for came.

"Hello," she answered on the second ring.

"Hi Laura. I just got back from my meeting."

"Did it go all right?"

"I think it did. Do you know when you'll be coming back yet?"

"No, I don't. When does filming begin?" she asked not remembering if Rob had told her yet.

"If things go according to plan we start filming January the fifth," Rob told her.

"I think that I'll go back on the second."

"Will you be flying or driving?"

"I think that I'll be driving. I'll rent a moving van.

"Keep track of how much you spend, and I'll reimburse you when you get here."

"Thank you."

"You're welcome."

They talked for the next hour and a half about memories from making their first movie, questions about the second movie and how the church was doing, before Rob, said that he needed to go.

To Rob's dismay, they never talked about anything personal. It was business as usual it seemed.

Laura spent the rest of the night reading over her script. She was going to enjoy her part in this movie.

Chapter 27

The next morning Laura slept in late. When she awoke at nine thirty, she read her devotional and then got ready to go to Bible study.

She was warmly welcomed back by the group.

"How have you been this week Laura?" asked Sandy, another Bible study attendee.

"I've been okay. I'm going to be in another movie this winter," she told Sandy excitedly.

"Really?" When?" asked some of the others.

"Filming starts January the fifth."

"That's just..." there was a pause to calculate, "That's three months away," Ami said in total surprise.

"What's the plot?"

"It's a detective story. There have been several petty robberies, so the store hires two private detectives. The only problem is, they tend to spend more time with each other than catching the thief."

"What's your part in this, Laura? Is it big or small?" this question came from Sally Copeland, Andy's older sister.

"I'm the detective's cohort."

"Congratulations."

The group then got started their study on the attributes of God.

When Laura arrived home, she found that her dad was not there.

She did, however, find a note on the kitchen table.

The note did not tell Laura much only that he had been invited to have lunch and would try to be home around one thirty.

Laura decided to call Andy to see if he would have lunch with her.

She dialed the memorized number but got only the answering machine.

Laura went to the refrigerator and fixed herself a salad; they had eaten all of the food that the church had given to them.

She was struck with a wave of loneliness.

While she ate she prayed. *Father, please help me to know how to deal with this loneliness. It seems to have come so quickly. Please be with me in the next few days.*

She continued to pray in this vein for the remainder of lunch.

After lunch, Laura studied her calendar.

She had only three months until she was to report to the studio.

It was hard to imagine that she was leaving again so soon.

She knew it would be the hardest to leave her father.

The last time she left she had known that she would see both of her parents again. Now she would not be able to look forward to coming home to her mom.

She couldn't contain her emotions any longer. She sobbed almost uncontrollably.

In the midst of her tears, Bill came home from lunch.

"Laura? Will you be okay?" he asked his daughter quietly.

"I will be," she told him with a sigh. "I was thinking about mom."

Bill nodded.

"How was lunch?" Laura asked albeit shakily.

"It was good. I went to Friendly's with Andy."

Laura nodded.

No wonder I couldn't get a hold of Andy. She thought to herself. "I feel like I should be doing something," Laura told her father, all of the frustration coming out in those words.

"I know what you mean. At the same time I don't know what to do either," Bill exclaimed, knowing exactly how she felt.

He missed Jeanette terribly. They had been married for nearly twenty-five years. In fact, it would have been their twenty-fifth anniversary in two weeks.

Laura's thoughts ran in the opposite direction. She thought about how long ago it had happened. As she thought, she realized that it had only been three weeks since it had happened. *So many things have happened*; she thought to herself. She began a mental list.

First, her parents had come, and then her mom went to the hospital. After that she had gone to the hospital and had surgery, then had found out her mom had passed away. To top it all off they had moved.

Laura felt exhausted just thinking about it. She yawned. To her dad she said, "I think I'll go take a nap."

"All right, I hope that you sleep well and feel rested when you wake," he told her, thinking he might do the same.

Bill thought of something as Laura left the room but decided that it could wait.

Thinking a nap sounded good, he sought out his own bed.

Laura had intended to take a short nap. However, things did not work out that way.

She slept for the rest of the day and all through the night.

Bill came in and checked on her a few times to make sure she was all right. The last time that he checked on her before he took himself to bed, Bill left a tall glass of water on Laura's nightstand thinking that she might be thirsty when she awoke.

Chapter 28

The next morning when Laura woke up she felt much rested but also disoriented. She didn't remember going to bed. She rolled over and looked at the clock. 8:30, she stretched and yawned contentedly. Laura thought she remembered that she had gone to sleep at eight thirty.

The next question that popped into her head was, is it morning or evening? She looked out her window and suddenly sat upright. It was morning. She had slept for twelve hours. Laura stretched again.

She got out of bed and went down to the kitchen to have breakfast.

"Good morning Laura," Bill greeted as Laura came into the kitchen.

"Good morning," she replied with a husky voice.

"Did you sleep well?" he asked with a laugh in his voice.

Hearing the sarcasm in his voice, Laura couldn't help but smile. "Yes, I did," she told him. "How did you sleep?"

"I slept well. Not as well as you did though apparently," he said with a wink.

"That's good," she decided to ignore the second part.

"Did I tell you that I got my next script in the mail?" she asked partway through breakfast.

Bill nodded. "Did you tell me how much longer you're here before you have to leave?" he asked sadly. He knew he would be lonely when she left.

"I'm not sure if I did. I leave in three months."

"I see… that isn't long from now."

"Will you be all right?" she questioned him.

"I will be, yes."

They ate the rest of their meal in silence.

During this time, an idea started to form in Laura's mind.

One that she planned to put into action.

That morning she made a couple of phone calls and by lunch time was ready to talk to her dad.

"I have an idea. Would you like to hear it Dad?"

"Sure. What's your idea?" he asked with an open expression.

"Remember how we said we wanted to do something but didn't know what?"

"Yes."

"I know what I want to do."

"What's that?" he asked knowing that whatever her thought was it was sure to be fun.

"I want to go horseback riding."

Bill thought for a moment.

"What does that look mean?"

Bill gave himself a mental shake. "I was just thinking. Do we still have stables around here?" he asked.

Laura nodded.

"Well," he said after a few more moments of thought," I think that sounds like a good idea. I haven't been riding since I was fifteen."

"I never knew you used to go horseback riding."

Bill nodded. "That's where I first asked out your mother. We both went riding that day and when we were grooming the horses afterwards we started talking seriously, and I asked her to go steady."

"Are you sure you're okay with going? I completely forgot that's where you two met."

"I think it would be a good way to remember her. How about we go at eleven o'clock and then maybe we can get something to eat afterwards?" Bill asked thinking it would give her enough time.

"That sounds great to me."

That morning, as Andy got ready for the day, he contemplated his schedule. As far as he knew, he wasn't doing anything, so he decided to go horseback riding. He knew it had been a long time since he had.

His plan was to go to the church for two hours to do some sermon preparation for Sunday. Then go to the stables and ride for an hour.

What has come over me? Andy asked himself as he walked out his front door. *I can't remember the last time that I've been so spontaneous.*

Laura's face came to mind, but Andy pushed the thought away. Grabbing his cell phone at the door, Andy determined to put Laura out of his mind.

In the early afternoon hours, before Bill and Laura had planned to go to the stables, time seemed to drag for both of them.

She had never had a chance to ride a horse before. She pretended to do house work but accomplished little.

Bill was not much better. He thought of the times that he had gone with his wife.

Laura's voice finally broke through Bill's thoughts. He realized that she had asked him a question.

"I'm sorry. What did you say?"

"I asked if you were ready to go. Are you sure you're okay with this?" she asked.

"I was just thinking about how I asked your mother to be my girlfriend at these stables," he told her quietly. "I still want to do this though. Are you ready to go?"

"I think so."

Just minutes later they were headed to the stables.

Andy got to the stables ten minutes before Bill and Laura, so he was able to see them before they saw him.

Laura wore a bright blue top with black jeans, and her hair was in a half ponytail. Andy thought that she looked lovely. *Your will be done, Father.* Andy prayed knowing that if Laura was back to stay he would lose his heart. He realized that he had always been attracted to her. Even in high school. Andy mentally shook his head. He slowly walked toward them, a smile on his face.

"Hello," he greeted them.

"Hello Andy," Bill greeted in return.

"I didn't know that you liked to ride," Andy said, his eyes turned to Laura.

Laura gave a small laugh. "I haven't actually been riding before today."

"I see. So how have you been doing?" Andy asked still talking to Laura.

At this point, Bill excused himself and went to rent their horses.

"I'm doing all right," Laura told him wondering if she should bring up the script.

The decision was taken from her hands.

"Well, I won't hold you up, I hope that you have fun riding."

"I will," she told him hoping for it to be true.

Andy walked away but turned when Laura asked, "Would you come riding with us today?" She suddenly realized that now was the perfect time to talk about high school.

"I would love to," he said with a smile.

Bill came back soon after this, and all three of them had a wonderful time together.

At one point, Bill told them he wanted some time to himself to remember all the good times he had here.

"Laura, I know it is soon after your mom passed away, but would you consider going out with me?" Andy asked hopefully, when they were alone.

"You mean like boyfriend and girlfriend? I wish you would have asked me about ten years ago. I had the biggest crush on you in high school," she said not answering his question.

"You did?" he asked in surprise. "I wasn't even nice to you in high school."

"I know. That's why I'm surprised that you want to date me now. What changed? You aren't at all the way I remember you. In fact, that's what I wanted to ask you about that night after we had lunch at Burger King. You never came. You didn't even call."

A tortured look came over Andy's face. "I stood you up! I was called on for a pastoral visit right when I was getting ready to come over and completely forgot afterwards. I am so sorry Laura. You must be wondering if I have changed at all."

"That actually is what I was afraid of that you hadn't really changed. I wish I wouldn't have jumped to conclusions, though. I never even thought about your having to pay a pastoral visit. I just assumed that; I wasn't a priority." Her voice dropped as she said, "That's how I felt in high school."

"I was completely immature back in high school. I thought it was important to be in the in-crowd, but I realize now that it was really lonely. It always looked like you had so much fun and maybe, I wished that I could have so much fun. I guess I was just jealous of you. You were living the life I wanted, but, wasn't bold enough to have.

"Then in college I finally got serious about my relationship with the Lord and I haven't been the same after that. Can you ever forgive me?"

"Oh, Andy. I waited a long time for this moment, so that I could tell you, I forgave you a long time ago."

"Wow. You are an amazing woman, Laura. I will do everything in my power to show you that you are very high on my priority list. So do I need to ask your dad's permission to date you?"

"I think that he would be appreciative of that but I'm old enough to decide whom I date," she said with a smile.

Chapter 29

Andy called Laura and now two days later they had lunch at the food court in the mall.

Laura went with a cheeseburger and fries, and Andy had a roast beef sandwich and fries.

They talked about general things for the first few minutes. Then Andy asked, "When does your movie come out again?"

"December fifteenth," she told him with a note of pride.

Andy smiled. "That's awesome."

Laura nodded. "I saw a preview for it on Tuesday," she told him with pleasure.

"Wow! That must be exciting. Are you in the preview?"

"Yes, I am. They even said my name when they were talking about who was in the movie," she told him excitedly. "I didn't think they would since I'm not the leading lady. They made mention that this was my first feature film.

"That's exciting. Are you going to be in another movie sometime?" Andy asked, not expecting the answer that he got.

"Yes."

"Really? When?"

"I leave for Hollywood on the second or third of January."

"That soon? Tell me all about it," he told her, excitement entering his voice.

Laura explained in detail the plot of the movie.

"And what is your role in this?"

"I'm the detective's sidekick."

Laura laughed at the expression on Andy's face," Don't look so shocked. Don't you think I can do it?" she asked in mock anger.

"It isn't that," he told her still amazed, "I just wasn't expecting that you would be leaving so soon. Congratulations, though, I am excited for you though."

Laura could see in his eyes that he meant it, "Thank you."

"Will you be working with anybody famous?"

Laura named a few that made Andy's mouth open in surprise. Laura laughed, and then told him in a serious voice, "Actors are people too. There's nothing special about us. We've just been given a gift. We all have gifts; yours is just different than mine is."

"Thank you Laura."

"For what?"

"Thank you for reminding me, that we all have gifts that we can use to reach others for God."

"You're welcome."

They talked for the next hour.

During that time, an idea kept coming into Andy's mind. He decided to call Bill to talk to him about it.

Andy didn't waste any time. After Andy had walked Laura to her car he called Bill, who answered on the second ring.

"Hello."

"Hi, this is Andy."

"Hi, what's on your mind?"

"Have you considered doing something to celebrate Laura's movie coming out in theaters?" Andy asked, hoping he wasn't out of line.

"She told you?"

"Yes, she did."

"The thought did cross my mind. What are your ideas?" Bill asked.

"I thought maybe we could rent out one of the theaters and invite the whole congregation to be there to watch her movie. What do you think?"

"I think that sounds like a great idea. I know Laura will love it.

"Okay, sounds good. Laura just pulled in the driveway."

"Okay, I'll see you on Sunday."

With that, both men hung up.

Chapter 30

The day had finally arrived. Laura was about to see her first movie. She was a bundle of nerves and excitement.

Rob called her after lunch.

"Hello," she said breathlessly.

"Hi, Laura," Rob said quietly over the phone.

"Hi, Rob. How are you?"

"I'm fine. I just saw the movie." he told her.

"You did? What time is it there?"

"It's just about two thirty."

"I'm going to see it tonight."

"Ah. You'll enjoy it," he told her with confidence.

"You were happy with it?"

"Definitely."

Laura's nervousness died right then. "Thank you Rob."

"For what?"

"I'll tell you later," she said looking at the clock.

"All right. Have you started memorizing your part?"

"I'm doing all right. How about you?" she asked with a smile in her voice.

"I'm doing all right. Are you excited about this movie?"

"I'm excited. I only have one question."

"What's that?" Rob asked.

"Are you a good actor?"

Rob laughed at that. "Yes, I can act. It won't seem that way though."

"Why is that?" Laura asked.

"I'm not going to tell you. You'll just have to see."

"Fine. I have to go," Laura told him smugly.

"What?" Rob asked incredulously.

"I'm going to the movies."

"Okay. Have a good time."

"I will."

Laura wasn't given time to think about her conversation with Rob. She had to get ready. Laura, Bill, and Andy were going to dinner before going to the theatre.

Andy arrived fifteen minutes earlier than planned.

Everyone was excited about the movie.

At the restaurant, they all ordered sandwiches but didn't eat much.

When they got to the theatre, Laura was in for a surprise.

Andy held the door open for Bill and her.

When Laura walked in the door, her whole congregation was there.

"Surprise," they all yelled.

"Wow, I can't believe that you're all here!" Laura exclaimed.

She turned to Andy.

"Did you do all this?"

"Of course I did," he told her, feeling proud of himself.

"Thank you," she said giving him a long hug and a kiss on the cheek.

"You're welcome, and thank you," he said returning her kiss. "I'll have to surprise you more often," he whispered in her ear.

People came up to her and asked her for her autograph.

After trying for a minute or two, Laura got the audience's attention. "I'd be happy to, sign autographs after the show."

Everyone agreed to this and sat down.

They all laughed and declared the movie a success.

There were even a few tears in the end.

"That was a great movie, Laura," Ami told her when she had the chance.

"Thank you," Laura said as she signed autographs for everyone.

"I'll talk to you later."

"Okay. Thanks Ami."

Laura continued to sign autographs for half an hour. Finally after everybody left, she too, was able to go.

"Thanks for being so patient," she said to Bill and Andy.

"You're welcome," they both told her. "Are you up for some ice cream, or some type of dessert?" Bill asked.

"A milk shake sounds wonderful," she told them realizing how thirsty she was.

They went to Friendly's, and all got chocolate milkshakes.

"This is good," Laura commented after a time of silence.

Both men agreed.

Bill could see that Laura was fading fast, so when he saw that she was done he paid the check and then they all left.

Laura was asleep five minutes after she got into the car. She was still asleep when they got home.

"Laura," Bill called gently.

Laura stirred and opened her eyes. She yawned, and slowly got out of the car. "Good night everyone."

"Goodnight."

Laura went inside and went to bed. It had been an exhausting day.

Outside Bill and Andy talked for a few more minutes before calling it a night.

Chapter 31

For Laura, the next few weeks were whirlwind of activity. She learned her part, did things with her dad, and went to Bible study and church. In her free time, she had phone conversations and e-mails with Rob, figuring out last minute details.

Christmas was difficult for Laura this year. Her mom had been gone for three months, and Laura missed her, terribly but, somehow got Christmas gifts for her dad and Andy.

Laura couldn't help but smile, every time she thought about Andy. He really had made her a priority in his life. Every day, they either saw each other or talked on the phone. It was so much sweeter than her childish fantasies in high school.

On Christmas Eve, Bill and Laura, along with most of the congregation went caroling. They all stayed up way too late, however, so Bill and Laura planned to sleep in the next morning.

That's why they didn't open presents until ten o'clock.

Laura was the first to awake, so she started the coffee and prepared breakfast.

"This smells good," Bill said as he came into the kitchen.

"Thank you. Merry Christmas."

"Merry Christmas to you too. What's for breakfast?" he asked.

"It's a breakfast casserole with hash browns, ham, cheese, and eggs. We also have fresh fruits."

"That sounds scrumptious."

"Thank you."

They quickly sat down to breakfast.

There was little conversation at the table because, both Bill and Laura thought of Jeanette.

Laura thought about the way her mom had gotten up so early every Christmas morning. No matter how early Laura had gotten up, Jeanette was already there.

Bill remembered the way she had always done the most thoughtful things. She would always let him sleep as long as possible.

Soon after breakfast they read the Christmas story as told in Luke. After a few moments of contemplation and prayer, they gave each other their gifts.

Bill gave Laura a twenty-five dollar gift card to the mall as well as a silver locket with a picture of Jeanette inside.

"Thank you Dad. I love it," she told him, tears coming to her eyes as she went to give him a hug.

"You're welcome," he said, tears coming to his eyes, as well. "Do you need help putting it on?"

"No, I've got it."

Then it was time for Bill to open his gifts. He received a framed 8x10 picture of Jeanette and him on their fifth wedding anniversary.

"Thank you Laura this is beautiful. Where did you find this picture?" he asked doing nothing to stop his tears.

"I found it in one of our family albums."

Both of them just sat there for a couple of minutes looking at the photos they had received.

"I guess that I'll put lunch on now," Laura said quietly.

Lunch was spent in laughter, because they had invited Andy to join them. After he had accepted he made sure, he wouldn't be interfering. It hadn't occurred to him right then that they had invited him, and not the over way around.

In fact, Bill told him just that. "If we hadn't wanted you to join us, we wouldn't have asked you."

"Merry Christmas Andy," Laura greeted as he came in the door.

"Thank you. Merry Christmas to you too. How are you?" he asked.

"I'm okay. How about you?" she asked.

"I'm doing pretty well."

"That's good. Are you hungry?"

"Very hungry," he said clutching his stomach.

"Good, lunch will be on the table soon," she told him with a smile.

"Can I do anything to help?" he asked.

"You could tear up some lettuce for a salad."

"Okay."

Before long they were sitting down to eat, and Bill led them in prayer. "Thank you Lord, for your many blessings, and thank you for the food that You have supplied and bless those who have prepared it. In Jesus name, amen."

"Feel free to help yourself," Laura told them after Bill's prayer.

They had a feast, with mashed potatoes, sweet potatoes, a seven-layer salad, deviled eggs, olives, and for dessert, chocolate pie.

The meal passed in fairly good humor; all things considered.

"What is the best part about being an actress?" Andy asked at one point in the meal.

"Let's see," Laura said as she thought, "I think my favorite part is getting to know the other actors and actresses."

"How many days do you have left?" this question came from Bill.

"Eight days," she told him in a state of surprise.

"That soon?"

Laura just nodded.

"Are you driving?"

"I'm going to drive. Otherwise, I wouldn't have transportation while I was there," she said.

"What is it like out there in Hollywood?" Andy asked with interest.

"It's hard to describe but I do have pictures in my room. I'll show them to you sometime," she told him, planning to do just that.

Andy nodded.

The three of them talked for another hour, and a half before Laura cleared the table. Andy was the first to give his gifts to Bill and Laura.

Laura opened hers first. It was a beautiful mahogany music box that played a tune from her movie.

"Where did you get it?" Laura asked in amazement.

"I know somebody who makes these," he told her simply.

"Thank you," she told him quietly, her voice full of emotion.

Bill opened his gift next. It was an antique pocket watch that still worked.

"Thank you, Andy."

"You're welcome. Merry Christmas,"

"Merry Christmas to you too," they both replied.

Then Andy opened his gifts; a beautiful silk tie from Bill and a bottle of expensive cologne from Laura.

"Laura, will you take a walk with me?" Andy asked after the wrapping paper had been cleaned up off the floor.

"I'd love to," Laura said as she went for her coat.

For the first few minutes, they didn't say anything but enjoyed each other's company. Andy stopped under a tree and pulled out a long slender box from his pants pocket. "I'm glad that you liked your music box, but there's something else that I wanted to give you."

Laura was curious and opened it up quickly. When she saw what it was she gasped. Inside was an exquisite gold necklace with a heart pendant. The heart was surrounded in diamonds. "Andy this is beautiful. I love it. Will you help me put it on?"

After the necklace was in place, Laura turned around to face him and saw that he was looking at her intently. She started to ask him about it, but Andy explained before she had a chance to ask.

"I love you Laura." For a second, she didn't respond, and Andy grew fidgety. "Did you hear what I said?" he asked uncertainly.

"I've waited so long for you to tell me that I was afraid you hadn't actually said it. I love you too, Andy. I think I have since high school."

With that, Andy took her into his arms and kissed her.

Laura thought that she could have stayed out there all night in Andy's embrace; but her teeth started chattering.

They both laughed. "We better get you inside the house."

Andy didn't stay a lot longer after they got to the house, but he promised to call the next day.

After Andy left, Bill and Laura went off on their own pursuits.

Laura did the dishes then took a nap.

Meanwhile, Bill sat in his favorite armchair and looked at the picture of Jeanette that Laura had given him. He missed her tonight more than ever.

Chapter 32

The week between Christmas and New Year's sped by for Bill, Andy, and Laura. She and Andy went out every night.

But for Rob the week felt like it would never end.

Laura had decided two weeks ago to drive instead of fly, which meant that he couldn't go to pick Laura up from the airport.

He told himself; it would be better that way because, Laura would be distracted and tired from the drive. No, it was better to see her the next day on set, so she was fully rested.

However, Andy dreaded the day that Laura left. He had just told her he was in love with her, and she was going to leave him.

He didn't have time to think about it during the last days that she was home; he was busy with plans for the party.

The plan was for everyone to meet at Andy's house for a "New Year's" celebration. Those who came were asked to bring light finger foods. Really, what they would be celebrating, was Laura's going away party. Andy knew that Laura wouldn't understand why she couldn't bring something, so he let her join in that part of the party planning.

When the list came around to Laura, she signed up to bring chocolate chip cookies.

All were excited.

Finally, the night arrived, and the plan went off without a hitch.

The ice cream cakes were thawing, the guests, except for Bill and Laura, were all there, and the decorations were hung.

All that was left was for Bill and Laura to arrive.

They got to Andy's house right at 10:00.

Bill, according to the plan, let Laura walk in ahead of him.

When Laura opened the door, everyone yelled, "Surprise!"

Laura looked confused. "What's going on here?" she asked as she looked around the room.

"We're giving you a sendoff party," Andy told her with a grin.

"Thank you," Laura said feeling stunned.

A minute later she was thronged with well-wishers. It was hard for her to take it all in.

She was slowly able to make her way towards the middle of the room and out of the entryway.

Andy managed to get everybody's attention.

"In a few minutes we'll cut the cake, so, if you'd all like to move that way…" he let the sentence hang.

Laura felt slightly overwhelmed as she walked toward the food table.

The evening was a wonderful affair for all who came.

In total thirty people came to wish Laura good luck and a good time.

In all of the excitement, Laura didn't get to thank Andy or even talk to him.

She had many good conversations with the others.

"Are you excited about going back to Hollywood?" Ami asked at one point.

"I am, and I'm not. I'm excited because I really like to act. It's fun to know that I'm entertaining people. I'm not excited about," here she paused and took a deep breath, "leaving my dad here; but I'm also not looking forward to being away from Andy."

At this point tears came to the actress's eyes that she made no attempt to cover.

"I wish I knew what to say. I'm sorry that this happened to you."

"Thanks."

"Was it hard to leave?"

"Not as hard as I expected."

At this point, somebody else came over and wanted to talk with Laura.

At five minutes before the year 2001, they turned on the television and watched the ball drop.

Soon after that everyone started to head home, giving Laura time to talk to Andy.

"Thank you for the wonderful party, Andy. I had no idea," she told him with a smile and a kiss.

"You're welcome."

"It's hard to imagine that I leave for Hollywood the day after tomorrow."

Andy nodded his agreement then asked, "What time are you planning to start?"

"I'm not positive, but I think that, I'll eat lunch here before I go. I'm not going to make the trip in one day anyway, so I might as well not pay for an extra meal."

"I'm glad that you get to sleep in a bit."

"Me too."

By now all of the guests had left, except for Bill.

"Would you like those last few slices of cake to take home?" Andy asked.

"Yeah, thanks."

"Did you have a good time tonight Laura?" Bill asked on the way home.

"I did. How long had the two of you been planning this?" Laura asked curiously.

"A couple of weeks."

Laura's eyebrows rose in surprise.

The rest of the ride home was spent in silence.

The next morning both Bill and Laura slept until ten.

"Good morning Dad. Did you sleep well?" Laura greeted Bill as he sat down at the table.

"I slept all right. How about you?"

"About the same."

"That's good. Did you have plans for today besides doing final packing?"

"No, I wanted my last day to be spent at home."

Laura told him with a touch of sadness.

Bill nodded in understanding.

That morning was filled with talking, packing, then more talking.

In some ways, Laura couldn't decide if she were looking forward to going back to Hollywood or not.

She was nervous about seeing Rob again. They had never officially started dating but how should she explain that she was dating somebody else?

Laura took several minutes to pray about the whole situation which she should have done a long time ago.

Chapter 33

The next morning dawned cloudy and gray. It matched Laura's mood perfectly.

When Laura entered the kitchen, she found that Bill had made a complete breakfast, of eggs, pancakes, and sausage.

"Good morning," he greeted her with a hug.

"Good morning," she said with a slight yawn trying to believe that it was a good morning. "Breakfast looks great. Thanks for making it, Dad."

"You're welcome. I didn't think that you should have to make breakfast for yourself this morning."

Laura responded by giving him a smile.

"What time were you planning to get on the road?" Bill asked.

After looking at her watch, she said, "Probably eleven."

Bill just nodded.

When they had finished, eating Bill helped with the cleanup.

"Do you need any help Laura?" he asked an hour before it was time to leave.

"No, I don't think so," she said as the phone rang.

Bill answered.

"Hello… Yes, she is. One moment, please," he then proceeded to hand her the phone.

"Hello?"

"Hi, Laura."

"Hi Andy. How are you?" Laura asked in surprise.

"I'm okay. How about yourself?"

"I'm okay," she replied.

"I know we've already said goodbye but I just wanted to say how much I'm going to miss you."

"I'm going to miss you too. But we'll talk every day. Right?"

"Absolutely. We'll figure out how to make our schedules work."

"I hate to say this but I have to go. I wish you could come with me."

"I wish I could too," he told her and meant it. "Know that my prayers and love are with you."

"Thank you Andy," Laura said with feeling. Then she added, "Thanks for everything."

"You're welcome. Well, I won't keep you longer. Good-bye Laura. I hope that things go well with your movie. I love you."

"I love you too. Goodbye."

Even after they said goodbye it was several seconds before either hung up the phone.

Not long after Laura hung up the phone it was time for her to leave.

"Do you have everything?" Bill asked before they left.

"I guess I do." Laura said looking around the house.

"Have a safe trip Laura," Bill said as he gave her a long hug.

"Thanks. I love you Dad. I'm going to miss you," Laura added tears coming to her eyes.

Seeing Laura's tears started Bill's. "I love you too Laura."

Bill watched as Laura's car pulled out of the driveway and cried for a full minute. Then he prayed; just as he and Jeanette had done the last time.

As Laura left the driveway, she looked back at her dad standing on the porch and wondered if she had made the right decision. Was she running away from her problems? As she did so often these days, she called Andy.

"This is a pleasant surprise," Andy said cheerfully when he saw who was calling him.

Laura didn't waste any time. "Andy, am I doing the right thing going to Hollywood right now? I feel like I'm just running away from my problems."

"Oh, Laura. I wish I was with you right now so that I could hold your hand all the way to California. I think you did make the right decision. God gave you this gift for acting; I think He would want you to use it. As for whether or not you're running away from your problems, I can't really tell you that. Did you pray about your decision?"

"Yes."

"What did you hear God saying to you?"

"That I should go. I just feel bad leaving you and my dad. I'm going to miss you both like crazy you know."

"You're sweet, Laura. Don't let me stand in the way of your dream though. Every time you have talked about making this movie, your face just lights up. You need to do this. I know that you would regret it if you didn't."

"I know. I guess I just needed to hear that coming from someone else. Thank you Andy. I'm truly blessed to have you as my boyfriend."

"Not as blessed as I am to have you as my girlfriend. I didn't deserve the second chance that you gave me."

"I've been given a lot of second chances too. If I didn't give you one, I would feel like a hypocrite."

"You do my heart a lot of good, Laura."

They talked for another hour about every topic under the sun.

When they got off, Laura turned on the radio and sang along with the praise songs until she stopped for the night.

By seven, o'clock the next morning, she was on the road intent on her destination.

For the first two hundred miles, the scenery was beautiful and made the trip manageable, even exciting. After that, it was grass and fields; much less exciting.

She only made stops for gas and meals and didn't stop driving until she made it to her old apartment in Hollywood.

A moment later she walked in the door. Home never looked so good.

Chapter 34

The first thing that Laura did when she walked in the house was to go to the couch and sleep for an hour and a half.

When she woke up it was a quarter to nine. Laura was hungry, so she meandered into the kitchen.

What am I going to do for supper? Laura wondered.

She opened the pantry in hopes that the previous renters had left something behind that she could eat.

She was amazed to find several boxed dinners. She also found a bag of her favorite potato chips.

A smile came to Laura's mouth as she decided to open the freezer door.

Laura's smile broadened when she saw that the freezer was filled with frozen dinners and her favorite strawberry ice cream.

Next she went to the cupboard and found even more groceries. Attached to a box of instant potatoes was a card which she decided to wait to open after dinner.

She went back to the freezer and picked a meal with chicken

and mashed potatoes. Just five minutes later, Laura sat down to her supper with a thankful heart.

Before long she was done with her supper, and she got out the card that Rob had given to her.

Dear Laura,

Welcome home! I wanted to let you know just how much I missed you while you were gone. I'm so glad that you're home.

I didn't want you to have to go shopping your first day back. So… I did it for you. Well, I just wanted you to know how much I love you Laura.

Love forever,
Rob

Laura smiled and reread the letter twice.

That was thoughtful of him. I wouldn't have wanted to go shopping tonight. Laura thought to herself.

She spent the next half hour thinking about what the future might bring. She found herself getting excited about that prospect.

She realized that she needed to tell Rob about Andy as soon as possible. She felt like she had led Rob on; but, at the same time she never remembered telling Rob that she loved him in return.

She just hoped that they could be friends because she did enjoy Rob's company. But it just wasn't the same as being with Andy. She hoped she could make Rob understand.

Chapter 35

Laura didn't get a chance to talk to Rob until the first day of filming.

She could hardly wait to see the actors and actresses who she would be working with a second time.

Laura also looked forward to this movie for another reason. She knew this movie would be fun because it starred Robert Lancing. The best part was that she was in most of the scenes which meant working closely with Rob.

Unlike her first day acting, Laura arrived at the studio fifteen minutes early.

She discovered that others were as excited as she was.

"Good morning Laura," Rob greeted her.

"Good morning. Thank you, Rob, it was wonderful to come home to find a kitchen full of groceries. I definitely didn't want to go out to eat last night."

Rob smiled and said, "You're welcome. How was the drive?"

"Even longer than I remember its being when I moved back with dad. How was your Christmas?"

"It was excellent."

Just then Cathy came to talk to her. "Hi, Laura. How are you?"

"I'm doing great. How about yourself?"

"I'm good. When did you get here?"

"I just got here last night. I'm excited about being in this movie. What's your role?" Laura asked curiously.

"I play the role of the bad guy's crony," she told her.

"Who's the bad guy?"

"Matt is," Cathy said in a warm tone.

Laura gave Cathy a knowing look and smiled, both which Cathy missed.

Laura laughed quietly and said, "So, how long have you known?" she asked bringing Cathy back to the present.

"How long have I known what?" she asked feigning innocence.

"How long have you liked him?"

Cathy realized at that point what Laura had been asking and answered, "I've liked him since the first time we acted together."

"Does he share the same feelings?"

Cathy nodded.

She would have said something except that Rob came over at that point to say that they would start filming in just a few minutes.

For Laura, the day of filming went by fast.

In the months, she had been away she had forgotten how much she liked to act. Of course, it didn't hurt that she got to alongside her best friends. She really hit it off with everyone in the cast and felt like they understood her in a way not everybody could.

Laura could see that Cathy was enjoying playing Matt's sidekick.

Before she left, Rob walked over to Laura and asked her what her plans were that night.

"I don't have anything special planned," Laura told him.

"Matt and Cathy are going on their first real date and they wondered if the two of us would like to join them. I think they're nervous about starting more than friendship."

"Sure, I'd love to come. What time do you want to go?"

"How about six thirty. Does that work for you?" Rob asked kindly.

"It sounds good to me."

"Great. I'll see you at six thirty then," Rob said before he was interrupted by a phone call.

Laura was excited about this evening. It would be great to hang out with Rob and Matt and Cathy.

Knowing that she was sure to be up later than usual she decided to take a nap so she could stay awake. She set her cell phone alarm clock and was asleep in seconds.

Rob left the studio and took a twenty-minute nap and then got ready to go.

By the time he got to Laura's house it was six fifteen.

He walked the few feet from where he parked his car to Laura's front door.

Laura saw Rob walking up the drive, so she opened the door just as he stepped on the porch.

"Hello, Rob."

"Hello, Laura. Are you ready to go?" he asked.

"I just need to get my purse and then I'll be ready," she told him as she headed toward the coat closet.

Laura was back shortly and asked, "So, what is the plan for tonight?"

"First we go to dinner, where we'll meet Cathy and Matt. Then if you feel up to it, we will watch a movie. Possibly dessert afterwards," Rob told her as he opened her car door. "How does that sound?"

"It sounds great to me," Laura told him enthusiastically. "Where are we going to eat?"

"There's a new Chinese restaurant on Main Street. Matt and I thought you and Cathy both liked Chinese, so we decided to go there."

"It sounds perfect."

In the space of five minutes, they were at the restaurant.

Matt and Cathy pulled into a parking space at almost the same time as Rob and Laura.

They were shown to a table and seated quickly.

Laura looked around at the décor with amazement. There were large Oriental tapestries and paintings all around the room. The walls were painted a warm creme and the floors were hardwood with rich oriental rugs. It was beautiful.

Her thoughts were interrupted by their waitress. "Hello, my name is Kim, and I'll be your server tonight. May I start you out with a drink?"

Rob and Matt ordered iced tea and Laura and Cathy both ordered hot tea.

"What are you having Rob?" Laura asked, undecided.

"I think that I'm going to have sweet and sour pork over fried rice and freshly baked rolls. How about you?" Rob asked.

Laura thought for a minute, then decided, "I'll have the teriyaki chicken over white rice," Laura said.

She decided none too soon. Their waitress came back a moment later to take their orders and bring them their drinks.

The night was filled with wonderful conversation, good food, and lots of laughter.

During the dinner, Rob realized how much he loved Laura. Then he started to think about when he first realized that he loved her.

Many times throughout the night Laura caught Rob staring at her. "That's a serious look," Laura said quietly for Rob's ears alone at one point.

Rob mentally shook himself and said just as quickly, "Ask me on the ride home."

Laura nodded.

Before too long, the bill was paid, and the four of them were headed to the theater to watch the last showing of their first movie.

This gave the four of them lots to laugh about, partly because of what happened on screen but also because of what they knew happened behind the scenes.

Laura enjoyed watching the movie with Rob, Cathy, and Matt. It seemed like it was funnier when she watched it with the people who had a large role in making the movie a hit.

It was decided after the movie that they should go get dessert from Friendly's before going home.

They all ordered hot fudge sundaes.

The two couples stayed up much too late considering the fact that all four of them had to be at the studio at 8:30 the next morning.

Chapter 36

When Rob dropped Laura off at her house both of them were reluctant to leave.

"Thank you for a wonderful evening tonight Rob," Laura told him.

"You're welcome Laura. I must say that I wouldn't have had nearly as good a time if you hadn't been with me," he told her sweetly.

Laura couldn't help the smile and blush that spread on her face. "Rob, I think that it is time for our talk now."

"Okay," he told her without a clue as to what to expect. "How was your time at home?"

Laura decided that this was a perfect lead in to what she needed to tell him. "I'm glad you asked. It was good. While I was there, I ran into an old friend of mine from school. His name is Andy. Actually, he's the one I told you about, that was mean to me in high school. Well, anyway, he's matured a lot since then. We started talking and hanging out, and now we're dating."

Rob was speechless. After a tense moment, he asked, "How could you do this to me?"

"I'm sorry Rob. I will never forget our time together as friends. We never did officially date," Laura said feeling horrible for having to say it that way.

"Well. I can't say I am entirely surprised. You never called or wrote me first while you were away. I should have known your feelings were not as deep as mine. Goodnight Laura."

He stood up to go, but Laura stopped him with a hand on his arm. Laura was sad that she had hurt him, but he needed to know the truth. "Is it possible to remain friends after this? I still want to have fun together and not hate every minute of making the movie together."

"We can try. Listen I need to go right now," Rob said.

On the drive back to his house, Rob thought about the fact that in a few months, Laura would go back home, and he would likely never see her again. He could do nothing to stop the tears from streaming down his face.

To Rob the next day of filming took a long time. It wasn't that he didn't enjoy being an actor. In fact, he had a wonderful time.

The reason for Rob's distraction, at least for part of the day was because he remembered his and Laura's last conversation.

Laura noticed that Rob was distracted and asked him about it.

He just shrugged it off and said, "I didn't sleep too well last night."

"I know what you mean," she said with an apologetic smile.

Okay Rob, get a grip on yourself. You have a job to do, he said to himself.

After his little pep talk, they all got back to work, and they all had a successful filming day.

That afternoon, Andy, made a call that would change his life.

He dialed Laura's old number, and she answered on the second ring.

"Hello."

"Hello, Bill?" Andy asked even though he knew who it was.

"Hey, Andy how are you?"

"I'm doing well. And how are you?"

Bill just sighed and said, "About the same as usual. So what's on your mind?" he asked adding, "I don't think you called to have a friendly chat."

"No, I guess not."

There was an awkward pause before Andy said, "This is hard to do over the phone. I want you to know that I love your daughter."

"I know. I saw it in your eyes when you came to see Laura at Christmas."

Andy continued, "I called to ask for Laura's hand in marriage."

"She's a special girl, so you take good care of her," Bill told Andy seriously. "As long as you treat her well and love her for the rest of your life and remain faithful to her, I'm happy to let you marry Laura."

"I will sir. Thank you," he said excitedly.

"You're welcome. By the way, there's no need to call me sir. I would much rather be called Bill. I guess in a few months you could even be calling me Dad."

"Thank you, Dad." He laughed in pure delight.

"When are you going to ask her?"

He thought about it for a while and then said, ",Not for a couple of months. I have to save up money for her ring."

"All right. I'll let you go now. Bye."

"Good bye."

They both hung up the phone a second later.

Andy's heart pounded with excitement. *She's going to be my wife!* He thought to himself. *Thank you Lord. Thank you for bringing her back into my life.*

Chapter 37

"Hello, Rob. How are you?" Laura asked in greeting.

"I'm doing okay. How about you? Are you doing well?"

Laura nodded and yawned.

They both smiled. "Did you not sleep well?" Rob asked compassionately.

"No, not really. I've just got things on my mind."

After a pause, Rob said, "I can't believe how fast the week has gone."

Laura looked confused for a moment. "What day is this?" she asked.

"Today is Friday," he told her with a smile.

"Time surely does fly when you're having fun," Laura said.

Rob surprised Laura with his next question, "Are you glad you came back?"

"Of course I am. Why wouldn't I be?"

Rob noticed that people had started to come in so he said, "Laura can we talk about this tonight?"

"Okay that sounds good to me."

A few minutes later Laura was busy getting ready for the filming to start.

The rest of the day went quickly for Laura and Rob.

Rob was at Laura's house early that night.

Fortunately, Laura was also ready early, so she was able to open the door as Rob came onto the porch.

"Hey, Rob," Laura said softly.

"Hi," he replied hands behind his back.

Laura smiled at the mischievous look on Rob's face.

Slowly he took from behind his back a dozen yellow roses and her favorite type of candy.

"What's the special occasion?" Laura asked in surprise.

Without skipping a beat, he told her, "There is none. Are you ready to go?" Rob asked after a moment.

"Let me put these in some water and then I'll be ready," Laura replied and entered the house to do so.

She was back after a minute and was ready.

Neither of them said anything on the way to the mall because traffic was heavier than usual.

They made up for it though once they got into the mall.

The two of them talked non-stop for the next two hours. Laura was surprised that things were not more awkward between them. She had thought long and hard before she agreed to go to the mall.

Chapter 38

On Sunday morning, Laura woke up at 6:30 and couldn't fall back to sleep. Church didn't start until ten thirty, but Laura got up and ready for the day.

She found that she was strangely more excited than usual. Laura had two hours to spend before she needed to leave.

After a time of wondering what she should do before going, Laura decided to put on a worship CD and just spent time reading her Bible and praying.

She was almost late getting to church that morning because she was so involved in the worship.

Rob experienced a similar morning. He was up at seven and felt wide-awake after only six hours of sleep.

He laid there for a moment or two asking God to have His way that morning.

After another moment, Rob clearly heard God tell him that the worship time for that morning needed to be longer than usual.

Rob laid there for a few more minutes before deciding to get up and make a relaxed breakfast.

The rest of the morning before church he spent preparing for the service.

Everyone came early all feeling the same anticipation that something good was going to happen.

Rob started the morning by saying, "Good morning. I'm glad that all of you could come today. This morning things will be done a little bit different. Before we begin let's pray. Lord, we commit this service to You. Do with it as You wish. Thank You for everything that You're going to do; in Jesus name, Amen."

After a pause Rob said, "This morning, I woke up earlier than usual, and I heard God telling me that we need to have an extended time of worship. So worship as the spirit directs you. You can sit, stand, lay down, dance, whatever.

"Let's worship this morning and not care what people think. This is God's time."

Indeed it was God's time. That morning God's presence was very real. Everyone who came that morning knew beyond the shadow of a doubt that God was real.

By the third song, Laura knew that she wasn't going to be able to stand in the presence of God for very long.

She had experienced this a few summers ago at a church conference in Canada, so she knew the signs. Some people referred to it as being slain in the Spirit; but Laura like to think about it as not being able to stand in the presence of God. She started swaying and felt such a warmth and peace come over her.

Laura started to lean forward and prayed. *God I don't mind falling but let me fall backward.* She had never experienced this outside of the conference she had gone to. There, somebody was there to catch you so that you didn't hurt yourself when you fell. So, after another thirty seconds she decided just to lie down on her own, not knowing if anybody would catch her if she did fall.

All of this took place in the space of two to three minutes.

Almost as soon as she was on the floor she experienced God in a whole new way.

God's presence was so real at this time. She felt God touch her tangibly. She could feel it on her left side and stomach. She felt the weight of His hand.

The best thing was that it was a gentle touch. It wasn't crushing by any means. Laura couldn't control herself. She started to shake. At first it was just a little twitch now and then. She felt more loved and cared for by her Creator than she ever had before in her life.

During this time, the music stopped, and they all stood in a circle holding hands and praying.

All of them stood except for Laura. She could not move. She felt like she was glued to the floor.

The two people on Laura's sides tried to help her to stand, but Laura told them, "No. Please, leave me where I am."

Hearing her tone of voice they respected her wishes and didn't try and help her stand.

Laura stayed like that for the next three hours which was another new thing. She had never felt his presence with her this long before.

She just laid there and enjoyed God.

Chapter 39

Laura had no idea how long she would have stayed on the floor if Rob hadn't eventually come back into the room.

Everyone had left except for her and Rob.

"Hello," he said softly.

"Hello," Laura said with a smile in her voice.

"Will you go to lunch with me?" Rob asked.

Laura blinked a couple of times and finally said, "It may take me a few minutes to be ready to go."

Rob smiled and nodded.

Laura slowly sat up and stretched. It was a few more minutes until she could stand and slowly make her way out to Rob.

The drive to the restaurant and ordering was somewhat of a blur to Laura. She barely tasted the food. She ate out of habit more than hunger.

Rob and Laura talked of general things during lunch.

This sort of surprised her but she didn't say anything about it. She wanted Rob to be the one to bring up what had happened that morning. She left soon after she had finished eating.

The next day at work was awkward.

It seemed to Laura that Rob wanted to talk about it but didn't know how.

So she just waited patiently.

Near the end of the day, Rob came up to Laura and asked, "Would you be willing to stay later than usual?"

"Sure."

"Great. I'll buy you dinner afterwards."

Laura had an idea of what Rob had in mind. She was right.

"Are you hungry?" Rob asked after the last shot.

Laura thought for a minute before replying, "Yeah, I am."

"Where would you like to go?"

"It doesn't matter to me," she told him honestly.

Just then Rob got a call on his cell phone.

He gave Laura an apologetic look then stepped a few feet away and answered. He was back in less than five minutes.

When Rob came back, he was all smiles. "Are you ready, ma'am?" he asked in his most chivalrous tone as he offered her his arm.

Laura couldn't help but laugh as she took his offered arm and asked, "Rob, what has gotten into you?"

"I will tell you sometime during dinner. That is all I'm saying on the subject at the present. Now shall we go?" he asked.

"All right," Laura said with another laugh.

Rob was jubilant all the way to Olive Garden.

They were quickly shown to a booth in the corner.

"What would you like to drink?" asked their waitress.

"I'll have sweetened iced tea, please," Rob told her.

Laura ordered hot tea.

"I'll be back with your drinks shortly."

"So," Rob began once they had their drinks in front of them, "Can you tell me what happened on Sunday?" he asked.

After taking a sip of her tea she started by saying, "Well that morning I just felt in my spirit that something amazing would happen."

She then proceeded to tell him all that she had experienced and ended by saying, "Always before God had revealed Himself to me as Father. Yesterday God revealed Himself to me as Lover. It was the best three hours of my life," Laura told him.

"Wow," Rob said when she finished. "That's awesome."

Laura nodded.

By now the food that neither of them remembered ordering arrived.

They sat there in silence. It wasn't an uncomfortable silence. It was simply a time to reflect.

Finally, Laura broke the silence by saying, "So, tell me your good news."

Rob mentally shook himself so that he could give Laura a sensible answer to her request.

"The phone call that I received was from a new production company. They're looking for somebody to play the main part. Apparently they heard about the movie that we're currently working on, and they want me to play the main character," he told her excitedly.

Laura was shocked as she heard that piece of news. "That's awesome. You're going to accept aren't you?" Laura asked her tone indicating what the answer should be.

Rob laughed. "I haven't decided yet. I'll have to pray about it and see what God's plan is."

They talked about it a few more minutes until their waitress came over and asked if they wanted dessert.

"I'll have a slice of your cookies and cream cheesecake."

"That sounds wonderful. I think I'll have the same," Laura told her cheerfully.

Rob and Laura talked almost non-stop for the next hour.

After checking his watch, Rob asked, "Would you like to take in an evening movie before I take you home?"

"I'd love to."

"Great," Rob said getting up to pay the check.

"One condition though," Laura said halting his moves. "Let me pay for the movie."

Rob tried to protest, but Laura stopped him and said, "You're always doing things for me. Please, let me do this for you. Besides we're just friends. I wouldn't feel right if you paid for everything."

He gave an exaggerated sigh and smile then replied, "How can I argue with that logic?"

"I guess you can't. What movie do you want to see?"

"Anything is fine with me."

After discussing their options, they decided that they wanted to watch something that was light-hearted and fun.

They eventually decided to watch a family movie.

Laura was glad they could remain friends.

Chapter 40

That same night Laura got home at nine o'clock.

She hadn't been home more than five minutes when the phone rang.

"Hello."

"Hi, Laura," answered her dad.

"Dad, this is a surprise. How are you?" Laura asked in amazement.

Bill laughed and replied, "I'm doing well. Why do you sound so surprised though?"

Laura laughed, as well. "I don't know. It's good to hear your voice," she told him seriously.

"I know that it's kind of late but could you give me your address?" he asked, arousing Laura's curiosity

"Why do you need my address?"

"I misplaced it. I searched all over the house but couldn't find it," he told her honestly.

"Oh. Okay," she said still a little curious. It wasn't like her dad to misplace things. She gave it to him anyway.

"Thanks," he replied after she had given it to him. "How's the acting going? Are you enjoying it?"

At this Laura came uncorked. She told him all about how long it would take yet, as well as some behind the scenes information.

She talked to her dad for the next hour and a half.

It was Bill who ended the conversation. "It sounds like you're doing well and enjoying yourself."

"I am," Laura said honestly.

"Good. Well, I need to be going."

"All right, thanks for calling me Dad."

"You're welcome. I love you."

"Love you too."

When Laura got off the phone with her dad she decided to go to bed, but not before reading her Bible and praying.

She read in 1 Kings 19:11-13 She read, The Lord said, "Go out and stand on the mountain in the presence of the Lord, for the Lord is about to pass by." Then a great and powerful wind tore the mountains apart and shattered the rocks before the Lord, but the Lord was not in the wind. After the wind, there was an earthquake, but the Lord was not in the earthquake. After the earthquake came a fire, but the Lord was not in the fire. And after the fire came a gentle whisper. When Elijah heard it, he pulled his cloak over his face and went out and stood at the mouth of the cave. Then a voice said to him, "What are you doing here Elijah?"

Laura closed her Bible and thought about what she'd just read. God had spoken to Elijah.

She found herself praying; *God do you still talk to people today?*

She turned out her light intending to go to sleep, but it didn't happen that way.

She started to think about how much she loved Andy Copeland.

Suddenly, a thought came to her mind, and she knew that it was from her loving heavenly Father who knew what was best. "I know the plans I have for you. Plans to prosper you and not to harm you. A plan to give you a hope and a future."

Laura fell asleep thanking God for his assurance and wondered if Andy were a part of that promise of a hope and a future.

Chapter 41

Andy decided to give Laura a call since she was settled in. She picked up on the first ring.

"Hello," Laura said happily. She recognized Andy's number on the caller ID.

"Hi Laura, how are you? Are you settled in yet? Sorry that I didn't call sooner, but I have picked up a second job." Andy said in a rush.

"I'm doing well. Just a few boxes scattered here and there. Why did you get a second job? Is something wrong with your car?

"No nothing like that, I just thought it would be best to start saving up my money. How is the movie coming?" Andy asked trying to distract her.

"It's going great. My coworkers are wonderful. The only problem is that there are a few romantic scenes between Rob and myself. I told him that we are just friends, and he is accepting it, but I didn't want you to find out by watching the movie."

Andy was surprised by the jealousy he felt for a moment; but, then realized that if there was ever to be a lasting relationship between the two of them he had to trust her. "Thanks for being straightforward about this, Laura. Do you mind if I come visit you soon? It is not to check up on you; I just miss you."

"That would be wonderful. I've missed you so much," Laura told him. "So you never told me, what is your second job?"

"I'm a waiter. I make pretty good tip money, so it's nice, and the hours are really flexible so I can still visit my parishioners and preach on Sundays."

"Good. Do you think you'll be able to get off to come visit me?" she asked anxiously.

"Yeah, I'll be able to get off from work. That isn't going to be a problem at all."

Just then the doorbell rang.

"Hold on a second Andy, someone's at the door."

"Okay, I'll hold on for as long as I need to."

When Laura opened the door, she squealed in delight. "Andy! You're here! How did you get my address?"

"I called your dad the other night and asked him for it. I missed you, Laura, and I just couldn't stay away from you."

"I'm so surprised to see you. When did you get here?" Laura asked after giving him a hug and kiss.

"Just about an hour ago. So are you going to invite me in?" he asked with a twinkle in his eyes.

"Oh. I'm sorry. Please, come in. Can I get you anything to eat or drink?"

"Not right now," he said as he settled onto the couch.

"Where are you staying? How long will you be here?"

"I'll be staying for three days. I rented a hotel room a couple of blocks away. Now then," he said patting the couch seat next to him. "Come and sit by me."

Laura was only too happy to comply. They spent the next three hours like that with Laura's head resting on his shoulder.

Rob was enjoying a Sunday afternoon nap when his cell phone rang and startled him awake. Mentally shaking his head he took a deep breath and answered, "Hello."

"Rob, this is Stewart Robinson from the Robinson and Son Productions."

"Good to hear from you again sir," Rob said remembering from the other night when he had been offered the acting job. He also remembered that Stewart had seemed friendly.

"Please don't call me sir. Call me Stewart. I don't believe we ever got an answer from you about the position. Have you made up your mind?"

"Yes, I have, I accept your offer. I don't have another project after I finish this one, so it works out nicely," he told Stewart. Besides, Rob thought to himself, I need to get away.

"I'm glad to hear it. Let's talk logistics for a minute Rob. While you're filming this movie, you'll be staying at a five star hotel all expenses paid."

Rob didn't know what to say.

Fortunately, Stewart just kept on talking. When Rob hung up the phone, he felt exhausted. Although he wanted to go straight to bed, he decided to fix a frozen dinner.

After he had finished his meal he slowly walked to his bedroom and lay on his bed thinking, he would just try to relax.

Within five minutes of Rob's head touching the pillow, he was sound asleep and slept through the whole night.

Chapter 42

The next morning Andy showed up at Laura's house with a bouquet of red and peach colored roses.

"Andy, they're lovely," she exclaimed with a smile that nearly split her face.

"Not half as lovely as you are my dear," he said and kissed her. She returned the kiss with enthusiasm.

When they pulled away, Laura blushed and invited him inside. "So what are we doing today?" she asked as she hunted around for a vase.

"Well, I've never been to Hollywood before; could you take me to see all the sights?"

"That sounds good to me. I never get tired of seeing the tourist locations. We'll have to do it after I get off tonight though. I'm filming until three."

"Oh. I see. I guess I should have called beforehand so you could have told me when you'd be working," he said with disappointment.

"Why don't you come with me? It would be so exciting to have you there, and I can introduce you to all the stars. What do you say?"

"That sounds great. I'd love to see where you work. Will Rob mind, do you think?" he asked wondering if it would be awkward for the two men to meet.

"Andy, Rob knows that we're just friends, and he's accepted that fact. Please come to the studio with me."

"Okay, I'll come. I just don't want you to feel awkward with me there but if you don't then I won't either. What time do we need to leave?"

Laura looked at her watch. "Right now. I didn't realize it was so late. Come on we'll take my car."

Forty minutes later they were at the studio. She introduced him to the cast but didn't see Rob anywhere.

"Andy why don't you sit here in director's seat for right now. He might tell you to move, but I'm not sure where else you could sit."

"Okay," Andy said with a grin.

Just then Rob walked in and was surprised to see someone new in the director's chair. He walked over and introduced himself. "Hi, I'm Robert Lancing, and you are?"

"I'm Andrew Copeland. I've heard a lot about you; it's great to finally meet you."

"Oh, so you're Laura's friend from back home?"

"Yes, I'm Laura's boyfriend," Andy said feeling strangely defensive.

Rob turned to the group that had gathered to watch what would happen. "Okay, people, this movie isn't going to make itself. Let's get to work."

Laura was right; Andy thought a few minutes later. *This is exciting to watch her in her element.*

However, just ten minutes later he wanted to change his mind. They were filming one of the romantic scenes that Laura had warned him about. It still made him uncomfortable though.

When the director finally yelled cut Andy was relieved. Laura came over to him right away. "So what do you think of the filming process?" she asked not noticing the way he looked uncomfortable.

"It's interesting. I have to say I'm very glad that you warned me about the romance scenes between yourself and Rob."

Laura finally caught something in Andy's tone and walked over to a quiet corner. After lowering her voice, she asked, "Andy, are you jealous? You have no reason to be. Rob doesn't mean anything to me. You're the one I love."

"I know. It's just not comfortable to see you like this is all."

"Do you wish that you hadn't come to see me making the movie?" she asked afraid that she had made a mistake.

"No. It's fine. We'll talk tonight over dinner."

"Okay. I love you Andy," she told him as she started walking back to the sound stage.

"I love you too."

The rest of the day went much better. Mainly, because there weren't any more love scenes being filmed that day.

Just as planned, Laura and Andy saw the sights and had a wonderful time. Andy's favorite part of the day was going to the walk of fame and seeing all the celebrity's hand prints and autographs. He was very surprised when his foot prints were very close to Tom Cruise's.

For dinner that night Laura took Andy to the Brown Derby where they debriefed about their day.

"Andy I'm sorry that you were uncomfortable at the studio this morning. I thought that Rob would be friendlier towards you."

"It's okay I was glad to see where you work. In truth, I enjoyed today. So please don't worry about me. I'm just fine."

They were both able to relax after that and enjoy their night together. They didn't stay out late because Andy had to catch a flight early the next morning. He didn't want to leave, but he wasn't able to take off many days.

Chapter 43

The last month of production was stressful for everybody. Rob and Laura were good actors, so they still acted well together, but everybody knew something wasn't quite right. Everyone was a little bit quieter than usual.

Nobody mentioned it though.

It was especially hard for Rob because of the upcoming move to New York to be in the next movie. The last week of filming was in some ways the longest and shortest week he could remember.

Before Rob was ready, the end of the week and production came. When the day was over they had a party. It was a party to celebrate the good work on another film and it was also to celebrate Rob's new job.

Laura stayed for most of the party but was still one of the first to leave.

Rob saw her go and, after excusing himself, went to go say a final good bye.

"Laura," he called to her.

Laura turned around. "Hello, Rob. Congratulations on getting the part. New York will be very exciting; I'm sure."

"Yes, the city is always exciting. Look, I didn't come after you to talk about my career. I have your last check here," he told her reaching in his pocket to give it to her.

"Thank you Rob. This past year and three months have been the best of my life."

"You shouldn't be thanking me. It should be me who should say thank you. I'll never forget you Laura. I love you."

Before Laura knew what was happening, Rob started kissing her.

She pushed him away. "What do you think you're doing?" Laura was furious.

"I thought that if we kissed one more time, that you might change your mind and choose me."

"Well you thought wrong! Rob, it's over between us. I love Andy." She walked away before he could reply.

When Laura walked away, it was one of the toughest moments for Rob. He wanted to run after her and make her change her mind. He knew he had been a fool. What had he been thinking? He had never done anything like that in his life. *Forgive me, Father.*

Rob took several minutes to confess and let go of the situation. It took him a while but by the time that he finished praying he could honestly say that he had put Laura in God's hands. That is where she always belonged in the first place.

When Rob was finally, able to give up control he was flooded with an incredible sense of peace.

He was finally able to go back to the party and enjoy himself knowing that he had nothing to worry about. He let out a huge sigh of relief.

As Laura left the building, she had mixed emotions.

Part of her was satisfied because she had done a good job on the movie. Another part of her was sad that it had come to an end.

She had enjoyed acting. More than she had expected.

For Laura acting was more than just a job. It was more than the pay check. As far as Laura was concerned, the pay was a bonus for having fun. It was a way to reach out to people. It was a way to make people laugh, maybe help them relax. Laura made sure that the characters she played were clean. She refused to do anything that went against the Bible.

She thought back to the end of her last movie. At that point, she had known that another job waited for her.

This time she had no such guarantee.

Then there was Rob. What could he possibly have been thinking, kissing her like that? She had never been so angry. She also worried that the whole thing was her fault in the first place. If she hadn't still been friends with him would he have been able to accept things easier?

She reminded herself that she wasn't responsible for the way that people reacted. She had done the right thing by telling Rob that she and Andy were dating. Rob was responsible for the way he handled that information.

Eventually, Laura got to her car and climbed in. She slowly turned the key in the ignition.

She took one last look at the studio, where the majority of the last year of her life had been spent. Even after everything that happened between me and Rob, it's still hard to leave. Then she gathered up all of her resolve and put the car in reverse and backed out of her spot, put it into drive and drove away. Laura went home and didn't look back.

Chapter 44

The following day Rob had some last minute packing to do. Most of his things had been put into boxes all that week, so it wasn't too hard.

The movers were coming that evening to pack his things into the moving van. He had debated whether he should fly to New York or drive. He weighed all his options. If he drove, he would have his car but be extremely tired when he arrived.

On the other hand if he flew he would be rested and he could take a taxi to places where he needed to go. Finally, he decided to fly, so he booked a flight for the day after the movers were scheduled to leave.

Rob went to bed early that night because he had to get up at five in order to get to the airport by seven. His plane was scheduled to leave at nine thirty.

Morning came quickly for Rob. He had a deep sleep that night and did not wake up until his alarm woke him.

Yesterday had been a big day for Rob, so when he boarded his first plane, bound for North Dakota, he slept the whole way.

Once the plane landed Rob had a three and a half hour layover. He spent part of that time watching TV. While there, he saw a commercial for the movie he had just been in.

It was bitter sweet to watch the commercial. It was of a scene that he and Laura had been in together. It was one of their favorite scenes.

Rob was deep in thought when somebody interrupted his reverie.

"You're Robert Lancing aren't you?"

Rob nodded.

"It's great to meet you," he said, then pulled something out of his briefcase and studied it. "I knew it," the stranger said a moment later. "Robert Lancing, I'm Jerry McCall. I'm going to be in the same movie as you when we get to New York."

Rob was speechless for only a minute. "Hey, Jerry look, I'm sorry that I didn't respond to you a moment ago. I was caught up in my thoughts. I hope you don't think that I'm stuck up," he told Jerry apologetically.

Jerry just shook the apology off saying, "Its fine. I understand we all have those kinds of days. I don't think you're a snob," he paused a moment then continued, "You're usually a producer right?"

"Yes, usually I am."

"Will it be hard for you not to have any say over this movie? I think I might have a hard time with that kind of switch."

Rob laughed. "It shouldn't be too bad. I've never been much of a control freak believe it or not."

Jerry smiled.

They sat in silence for a few minutes before Rob asked, "What's your row number?" he asked curious to see if they were seated near each other. Rob thought that if they were it would help to pass the time.

"My ticket is for row 2B

"I'm in row 2A."

"That's cool. So, where are you from originally?"

"I was born in Florida but spent most of my life in California. Where do you call home?" Rob asked in return.

"I was born and raised in North Dakota. I got into acting during college, and it just snowballed from there."

"Have you ever been in a movie before?"

Jerry nodded.

Rob and Jerry talked off and on for the trip to New York. Rob had been starting to stress about his situation, but he now found himself relaxing.

For Laura, the next few days turned into a type of routine. She got up early and listened to worship music then read her Bible.

Then she would get up and go about her day joyfully. One day she decided to call her dad. She realized that she hadn't told him about what happened to her during church the other week.

Bill answered on the second ring. "Hello."

"Hi, Dad, how are you doing?" she asked.

"I'm doing well. How are you doing?"

"I'm doing okay," Laura replied.

"I'm glad to hear it. So, what's going on Laura? It sounds like you have something to tell me," Bill told her with a slight smile in his voice.

"You know me too well don't you Dad?" Laura said with a smile.

Laura proceeded to tell her dad all about what happened the previous Sunday and how Andy had come and surprised her two days ago.

When she finished her story, Bill gave a short laugh and said, "Wow, sounds like you have been having an exciting time. Did you have fun with Andy?

"Of course I did. It was so wonderful for him to surprise me like that. We didn't have nearly enough time together though. Have you considered moving anymore or was that just an initial idea?" Laura asked nervously.

"Well, honestly, I had planned to call you today, because I listed the house, and I have a meeting with my realtor to show me some houses."

"Oh… I can't say that it surprises me too much. Will you move into a smaller house?"

"Yeah, I thought I would look for just two bedrooms and one bath." Bill replied.

"Well I hope that it goes well for you today. I think that I know the answer but… can I come home?" she asked almost hesitantly.

"Oh, Laura," Bill sighed. "Of course you can come home. You didn't even need to ask."

"Thanks. It's just that I thought I might be wearing out my welcome since I have graduated college and have been living on my own."

"You could never wear out your welcome."

"So, are you planning to stay local?"

"I am. I love the people here too much too say goodbye to them completely. Besides, I think I probably need all the connections I can right get right now."

"That sounds like a wise decision," Laura said, inwardly praising God. "Well, I should probably start packing."

"All right, well, thanks for calling. Good-bye Laura I love you. Have a good day."

"You too Dad. I'll get there on Monday or Tuesday of next week."

"All right."

A moment later, Laura was off the phone. She went to the family room and sat in her favorite chair to think. Her dad's news took her off guard more than she thought it should. *God help my dad and me to make this time of transition to move forward. I still miss my mom so much, Lord. I'm usually too busy to acknowledge it though. Help me to slow down and take the time to deal with everything.* When Laura finished praying, she felt much better.

Chapter 45

Rob was amazed by the housing that the studio provided him. He stood just inside his hotel suite. He had a kitchenette including a stove, refrigerator and dishwasher, a living room filled with couches covered in Italian leather and an office that was bigger than the one he had at home.

The view from his window took his breath away. There was a courtyard with a fountain and a beautifully landscaped garden. The predominant flowers were tiger lilies. Laura's favorite. Rob remembered her telling him about how her grandfather used to grow tiger lilies and how much she used to enjoy seeing them.

He shouldn't have been surprised though. Everything he saw reminded him of Laura.

Rob sighed and decided the best thing to do would be to go to sleep and try to forget.

But, before he did that he set his travel alarm clock. Tomorrow he started acting. That night he prayed for his coworkers and his boss. He prayed that they would all work together and not fight.

The next morning when Rob's alarm clock went off he woke up feeling disoriented.

He soon remembered and sat up in his huge bed. He could hardly wait to go to the studio this morning.

He quickly got dressed then walked around his house exploring and trying to think what he would do with his things.

When he got to the kitchen, he found that the pantries and the refrigerator were empty.

I'll have to go shopping this evening. Rob thought to himself.

He decided to pick up something on his way to work at a fast food restaurant he knew he would pass to get to the studio.

He left the house at seven thirty so that he could get to work by eight fifteen.

However, he didn't account for the rush-hour traffic. He ended up being half an hour late. This brought to mind the first day Laura came to work at the studio late.

He had to smile at the irony, about how Laura had come in late and how he reacted and how he could definitely understand how nervous she was that first day.

Rob was met at the studio door by his director Jack Smith.

"What happened to you, Rob?" he asked, not unkindly.

"I'm not accustomed to the New York traffic. I'm sorry sir."

"There's no need to call me sir. You're a Christian aren't you?" Jack asked.

"Yes, I am."

"So am I. It's great to have another Christian brother here on the set. There are so few," Jack added.

Rob nodded in agreement.

"Well, good talking to you Rob. I'd love to talk longer, but we've got to get started soon," he told him.

"I understand. I'm sorry that I was late," Rob apologized again.

Jack just shrugged. "It happens to everybody. Now go to wardrobe and get back to the sound stage."

Rob nodded with a smile and went to do as he was told.

Two days later Laura once again packed up all her belongings, arranged them in the car, and prepared herself for the long trip home. She was ready though. It was time to go home.

She needed to see her dad and her church family. She hadn't realized how much she had missed her dad until she had talked to him on the phone, the other day.

Laura drove about ten hours a day and would make fairly frequent stops to get things to eat or drink to help keep her awake.

It took Laura two days to travel from Hollywood to her home in Dallas, Texas.

After being on the road for so long, home never looked so good.

Laura yawned as she got out of her car and walked to her front door.

When Laura stepped onto the porch, her dad was there to welcome her home with a big bear hug.

"Welcome home Laura. I've missed you," Bill said with a catch in his voice.

"Thanks Dad. I've missed you too. How are you?" Laura asked.

"I'm doing all right," he replied.

Something about his tone that made her doubt that, but she didn't comment.

"You must be exhausted Laura," Bill commented about five minutes later.

"Yeah," Laura said on a yawn. Then with a smile she continued, "I got up at six o'clock this morning."

"Would you like some dinner? I made chili and rice."

"That sounds good."

Laura finished her supper at seven o'clock. She started to clean up the kitchen, but Bill stopped her.

"Just go to bed. I'm sure you'll sleep the whole night."

Laura smiled and nodded. She took her suitcase and went to the bedroom that had been hers for most of her life.

She was glad that nothing had been done to change her room. She sat down on her bed and smiled contentedly.

The room was a bit chilly, so she changed into a pair of sweatpants and a sweatshirt, and then crawled into her bed.

When Bill checked on her ten minutes later Laura was fast asleep.

After he checked on Laura, Bill read a book for a while but he quickly lost interest.

He was so lonely most of the time.

He sighed, and decided just to go to bed rather than think about his present situation in life.

Both father and daughter slept until nine o'clock the next morning.

They both got to the breakfast table at the same time.

"Good morning Dad," Laura said, fully rested from her long drive.

"Good morning Laura. Did you sleep well?"

"I slept wonderfully. I don't remember the last time I slept so long. It was great to be in my own bed. How did you sleep?"

"I slept well. I woke up once or twice. So what would you like for breakfast?" Bill asked.

"What do you have?"

"Pancakes, waffles, eggs, bacon, sausage, and hash browns," he replied with a smile.

"Wow! Let's see, how about hash browns, eggs, and bacon," Laura said impressed with her choices.

"Why don't you go and get ready for the day and I'll make some breakfast," Bill suggested.

"Thanks Dad. It's so good to be home. Do you mind if I do a load of wash?"

"Sure go ahead, any time you want."

Laura took a shower and was back in the kitchen half an hour later; a towel wrapped around her hair.

She sniffed the air appreciatively. "Breakfast smells wonderful Dad."

"Thanks."

They ate amid lively conversation.

When they were about half way through breakfast, the phone rang. "I'll get it," Bill said and got up to answer it.

He was back in a few minutes and said, "Laura the phone's for you."

"Do you know who it is?" Laura asked curiously.

"It's Lindsey."

Laura nodded and went to get the phone. She was an old friend from high school that she had not heard from in years.

"Hello?"

"Hi Laura, how are you?"

"I'm doing well. How are you?"

"I'm doing well. I know that you just got home, but would you like to go to lunch with me today?"

"Sure, I'd enjoy that. Where and when?"

"How about twelve thirty at Friendly's?"

"That sounds good."

"I'll see you then. I have to get back to work."

"Okay. Thanks for calling. Bye."

"Bye."

Chapter 46

Laura and Lindsey pulled into parking spaces at the same time. "Talk about timing," Laura said with a smile.

The two women hugged. "So are you home for good?" Lindsey asked.

"I'm considering it. I can't say that I would miss the big city. Besides I don't have anything to go back to," Laura said as a matter of fact.

They were seated a few minutes later.

"Where are you working now Lindsey?" Laura asked after they had gotten menus.

"I'm working for a daycare."

"Do you like it?" Laura asked with interest.

Lindsey nodded, and then asked with a rather mischievous smile, "So, Laura how is your handsome producer friend?"

Laura smiled and replied, "I agree that Rob is handsome. There's no denying that. So on that part you're right. However, he is no longer mine, and I don't know how he is."

Lindsay opened her mouth to say something but didn't get the chance.

At that moment, their waitress came to get their orders.

As soon as she left Lindsey exclaimed, "Laura why? I saw you two. You looked like you were in love. What happened?"

Laura explained by telling her friend that it was all a part of the role she was playing. Her heart belonged to Andy Copeland. She wanted to make it clear to her friend that even though she was in love, God still had to come first.

"God is sufficient. I don't need anybody else. If God allows a future with me and Andy then that will be wonderful. But if not, I'm sure that God will give me something even better."

After she finished lunch with Lindsey, Laura called Andy on her cell phone.

"Hey, Laura. Welcome back. How was your drive?"

"Andy it's great to talk to you. It was fine; traffic was smooth most of the way. So are you still working the second job?"

"Yeah, but I'm hoping I don't have to work there too much longer. Will you have dinner with me tonight?"

"Of course. What time? Should I dress up for the occasion?"

"Five thirty and yes you should definitely dress up. You and I are going out on the town tonight."

Laura smiled at his tone and said, "I can hardly wait."

They talked of general things for the next three hours. It didn't matter what the topic of discussion was. Just knowing that they were finally back in the same town was enough.

Andy arrived right on time dressed in a suit and tie and holding more flowers and chocolate truffles, Laura's favorite kind of candy.

They greeted each other with a passionate kiss and then Andy took her hand and led her to his waiting car.

"I've missed you so much," he told her quietly.

"I've missed you too Andy. So much has happened since the last time I saw you."

"I know. We'll have to catch up over dinner."

"Speaking of which, where are you taking me anyway? You know I just absolutely, hate surprises," Laura asked trying her best to sound annoyed. She failed miserably.

Andy just smiled. "What do you mean? You love surprises," he said matching her tone of voice perfectly. "I'm afraid that I can't tell you that, and I must insist that you wear this blindfold."

Laura looked suspicious but did as she was told.

Twenty minutes later the car came to a stop, and Andy helped her out of the car.

"Can I take off my blindfold now?" Laura asked with no idea where she was.

"Yes you may."

Laura was shocked to open her eyes and see that they were at the lake with a candle lit picnic dinner awaiting them. "Andy, this is amazing. How long have you been planning this?"

"It's been about a week since I thought of this," he told her, pleased by the look of pleasure in her eyes.

After they settled onto the blanket Andy asked casually, but trying to show that he cared, "So how's Rob doing? Did you like acting with him or was it awkward?"

"I actually did enjoy acting with Rob. He's good at what he does," Laura said after a slight pause.

Andy considered asking if Laura thought she would be in another movie in the future. Right as he was about to ask her, he looked at her face and saw sadness with something else and decided against asking her. She would tell him when she was ready.

"I have to tell you something about Rob."

"Okay."

He kissed me the last night we worked together. I shoved him away as soon as he started kissing me."

"I see. Do you still have feelings for him?"

"What does this tell you?" Laura asked as she kissed him passionately.

Andy laughed when they pulled away. "Hmm, I don't know. I think I could use some more convincing."

"Oh, you do, do you?" Laura asked.

Andy just nodded. Laura was more than happy to oblige.

"I think we better change the subject before we get too distracted. So, how is the church? I can't wait to come on Sunday," Laura said to fill the void.

"It's going good really. God is starting to move in the church," Andy told her with excitement in his voice.

He went on to explain how people were becoming freer in their worship.

Then Laura told Andy about what she had experienced in church in Hollywood.

After they ate dinner, Andy asked if she would care to go swimming.

"What exactly are you suggesting my good sir? I didn't bring a swimsuit."

Andy shook his head. "Do you really think that I would put so much thought into this and then forget a swimsuit for you?" He took her to the car, opened the trunk and took out a bag of bathing suits. "I didn't know what size you would need, so I got several just in case," he said looking slightly embarrassed.

"Oh, Andy. I love you."

"I love you too."

They kissed for such a long time that they almost forgot that they meant to go swimming.

The rest of the evening passed much too fast for both of them.

Hollywood California 6 months later

On the day Rob flew home from New York he was greeted by his small church family at the airport.

"Welcome home, Rob," Matt said enthusiastically.

"Thanks. It's great to be back."

"Are you tired?" Cathy asked.

Rob had a feeling there was more to the question. "I'm a little tired. Why do you ask?"

"We're having a welcome back Rob party at my house. Are you up to it?"

"Sure. I'd love to come. When do you want me there?"

"Come in two hours."

"All right. I'll see you then."

When Rob got in the car, he thought about his latest production venture. It would start in five months. He was also the talent scout again.

He pulled out his cell phone and dialed the number of somebody he had met during his last movie. She had been an extra but Rob saw potential.

The name of the actress was Lois McMurray.

Chapter 47

Chicago Illinois

It was three thirty when Lois McMurray got Rob's phone call. She looked at the caller id number and saw that it was from Los Angeles.

"Hello," Lois said hesitantly.

"Hi, is this Lois McMurray?" Rob asked.

"Yes. May I help you?" Lois asked still not recognizing the voice.

"This is Robert Lancing from the Lancing Production Company. I wondered if you would like to be in my next movie," Rob said waiting until Lois said something.

Lois was stunned. The only thing she could thing to say was, "How did you find out about me?"

"I saw your application at a national producer's convention. Are you interested?" Rob asked again.

Lois finally responded saying, "I would be very interested."

"Great. I saw your video, and it looks good."

"Thank you."

They talked for a few more minutes and then Rob said that he needed to go.

Lois just stood and looked at the phone for a few seconds after Rob had hung up.

Finally, she noticed that she was still holding the phone and pushed the off button.

She had always wanted to be an actress. As long as she could remember that's what Lois had wanted to do. Now she would finally get her chance.

As she processed the information, a huge smile stretched across her face.

Rob felt great relief when he hung up the phone after talking to Lois. He hadn't anticipated that she wouldn't accept, but it was still comforting to know for sure.

Rob's next thought was of Laura Johnson. This was harder than he had expected.

He missed her, missed talking to her. He missed being able to take her to dinner or to the movies.

Rob sighed loudly and wondered how long it would be until he stopped feeling the way that he did. He wondered if he would ever see her again.

It took Rob a full half hour to get his mind off of Laura and onto the work that needed to be done. Then when he did focus on his work he was only successful for a few minutes.

He sighed as he looked at his watch and saw that it was 8:30 in the evening. He let out a large yawn and decided to go home and go to bed. At least when I'm asleep I can escape my thoughts. Twenty minutes later Rob was fast asleep.

Lois McMurray couldn't sleep. Soon after she had gotten off the phone with Rob she called her mother, Sarah, and told her all about her conversation with Rob.

Sarah then asked if it'd be okay if she came for a visit.

Lois told her that it sounded okay to her, but she wasn't entirely sure that she wanted her mom to come.

The last time that she and her mom were together they had argued about religion. Lois simply didn't get it. How could you believe in something that you couldn't see? Her dad had died in a car accident when Lois was sixteen years old.

Sarah was a Christian at the time, and she stayed strong, she said, because of her faith.

Lois didn't share her mom's faith. She got mad at God that her father was taken from her.

She wasn't sure that she wanted to discuss this with her mom.

Lois looked at her alarm clock and saw that it was a quarter after twelve. She yawned and finally fell asleep.

Chapter 48

Laura needed something to do. She had been home for months now, and she was getting tired of packing for the move across town. The only good thing was that it would be closer to Andy.

Suddenly, Laura remembered Andy's lunch invitation.

Quickly she dialed his number.

"Hello," Andy answered on the second ring.

"Hi Andy. It's Laura."

"Hi, Laura. How are you?" Andy asked trying to sound as normal as possible.

It had been a week since they had seen each other. They had talked on the phone every night, but somehow they didn't see each other. They had gotten extremely busy and hadn't had time to connect like he thought they would. He had thought about their relationship. He knew that he loved her and was ready to take the next step.

In fact, he had just gotten back from buying her engagement ring. Andy thought he would wait a few more weeks though, so he could plan something extra special.

Laura's voice broke into Andy's thoughts, and she said, "I'm doing okay. I wondered if you would have lunch with me today. I'm feeling cooped up with all of this packing."

"I'd be glad to go to lunch with you today. Name the time and the place," Andy said happily.

Laura did and then they both hung up the phone.

They were to meet at Bob Evans in twenty minutes.

Chicago

Sarah McMurray's plane arrived twenty minutes later than expected. They had experienced a lot of turbulence.

While exiting the plane, Sarah prayed for guidance. She determined not to bring up anything that had to do with God. Her reasoning was that the more she argued with her daughter, the more Lois would reject it.

Sarah came to that conclusion not a moment too soon. Just as she had decided that, she stepped off the plane and was met by Lois.

"Lois, good to see you. How are you?" Sarah asked as she gave her daughter a hug.

"I'm doing okay. How about you?" she asked returning her mom's hug.

Both were somewhat surprised that Lois's hug was sincere.

They were silent as they made their way to pick up her mom's luggage. It took a few minutes before they found Sarah's luggage but eventually they did.

On the way to the car Lois asked, "How long can you stay?"

"I planned to stay for about a week. Is that okay with you?"

"Yeah, that's fine. Are you hungry?"

"No. They fed us on the plane. Have you eaten yet Lois? If you haven't I could just sit there with you," Sarah suggested.

"I am hungry but I'll just go through a drive through somewhere."

"Okay."

There was a pause and then Sarah said, "Lois, I'm very proud of you. I know that you will do well in Hollywood. I'm just sorry that your father isn't here to see you."

Lois was silent for a moment and then didn't know what to say, so she just gave her mom a hug and said, "I know Mom. I miss him too. I guess that's something that will never change."

Laura was the first to arrive at Bob Evans. Fortunately, she didn't have to wait long. Within ten minutes, Andy stepped out of his car.

"Hi Laura. How are you?" Andy asked as they walked inside together hand in hand.

"I'm doing well. How are you?"

"I'm doing all right."

"Thanks for coming to lunch with me Andy," Laura said when they were seated at a table for two.

"You're welcome."

They sat in silence while they looked at their menus and decided what to order.

There was a short wait before their waitress, Julie, came and asked if they were ready to order.

Laura looked at Andy and nodded that she was ready and knew what she wanted.

"Yes, I think we're ready to order. I'd like water to drink and then I'd like the meat loaf with mashed potatoes and corn. What would you like Laura?"

"I'd like a hamburger and fries and pink lemonade please."

"I'll be right back with your drinks."

After their waitress, left Andy tried to keep the conversation on lighter topics. He felt too distracted by knowing that he wouldpropose to this special woman soon.

Laura seemed content not to discuss anything too deep.

"I'm so glad that we found each other, Laura. I cherish your friendship. Whenever I start to feel anxious about anything, you know exactly what to say to set me at ease."

"I feel the same way about you."

For the next hour, they simply enjoyed each other's company.

Andy left feeling captivated by Laura and couldn't wait to see what all God had planned for them. Whatever it was, he knew it would be good, because Laura was part of his life.

Rob felt undone the first day of making the new movie. He missed Laura and didn't know what to do.

He purposely kept himself busy to keep his mind off of her.

He was relieved that all of his actors were there on time.

This will definitely be interesting. Rob thought to himself.

Chapter 49

Lois' first day as an actress was exciting and scary. It was everything that she thought it would be. She didn't know any of the other actors, but they seemed to be nice.

Rob wasn't what she expected. He seemed to be preoccupied, but he was still kind.

Lois' mind drifted to the past week that she had spent with her mom. It had gone better than she had expected. They had resolved a lot of their issues and had been able to enjoy that week.

By now it was six o'clock and Lois was hungry. She didn't have a lot of food and so she decided to eat out at a restaurant that a couple of her fellow actors had talked about.

Rob was tired after a long day of directing. He looked at his watch and realized that it was time to eat. He didn't feel like eating and knew that if he went home he wouldn't eat much.

He had heard about a new restaurant opening on Hollywood Boulevard and decided to check it out.

Both Rob and Lois went to the same restaurant to eat that evening.

Rob got there ahead of Lois and had just sat down to order a Pepsi to drink when he saw Lois come in the door.

He saw that Lois was being seated in the booth right in front of him. He didn't think that she had seen him yet. Rob thought for a bit and decided to ask Lois to join him so that neither of them had to eat dinner by themselves.

Rob got up and stood before Lois's table.

"Hi Lois."

"Rob, hi. How are you?" Lois asked surprised to see him.

"I'm doing all right. Would you like to join me at my table? I'm sitting right behind you," Rob told her in explanation.

"Oh. That sounds good. Thanks Rob."

"No problem. It doesn't make sense for us to eat by ourselves."

When Lois's waitress came back with her drink, she was surprised to see that Lois had changed but quickly recovered and delivered her drink.

The two made small talk until they got their dinner order of hamburgers and milkshakes.

"So tell me about yourself," Rob said as he dipped a French fry in catsup.

"Let's see..." Lois said not knowing where to begin.

Rob jumped in and helped. "Tell me about your family. Do you have siblings? Where did you grow up? What are your parents like? Does that help?" Rob asked with a smile.

"I'm an only child, but I'm not spoiled by any stretch of the imagination. My parents definitely taught me to put others ahead of myself. My dad was a pastor for six years, but he died in a car accident when I was a teenager. Since then I haven't been very happy with God. I mean; I believe that God exists but I struggle with whether God is involved in our lives."

Lois paused and took a long drink of water seemingly gathering her thoughts. "Most of my schooling was in Chicago where I graduated from a Christian school. Then I went to a community college and majored in acting and dancing. So, tell me about yourself," she said, wanting to get the attention off of herself.

"Well, I grew up in Florida. My dad was, as long as I can recall, interested in movie making. When I was eight, my dad started a production company. He always wanted me to run it with him one day. He died when I was fourteen. Mom remarried three years later; but I've come to love him as my dad. When I was nineteen, I took over the business."

"Did you want to be something other than a director?" Lois asked in curiosity.

"No, not really. I've toyed with the idea of writing a movie, but I've always been fascinated by movies. I was especially fascinated by the special effects and always tried to figure out how they did it. How about you? What made you become interested in acting?"

"In high school I always starred in the plays. My school did plays like *Fiddler On The Roof* and *The Sound of Music*. Everyone said that I did a good job. Ever since then I've been looking for any opportunities to act. When I found out about the production conference I sent in my audition tape," Lois said. She smiled and said, "And then of course, you know the rest of that story."

Both were nearly done eating their dinners.

"Do you want any dessert?" their waitress asked when she came to their table.

"That sounds good. I'll take a chocolate ice cream cone, please," Lois said with pleasure.

"How about you?"

"I'll take the same," Rob said thinking how tempting that sounded.

"All right. I'll be right back with your orders."

Rob and Lois talked about general things while eating their ice cream.

Lois looked at her watch and was surprised to see that it was already eight o'clock.

"Is something wrong Lois?" Rob asked seeing the expression on her face.

"Oh, it's nothing. I was just surprised that two and a half hours have passed," she replied with surprise.

"Really? It doesn't seem like it's been that long," Rob said also feeling surprised.

"I should go," Lois said as she picked up her check.

"I should get going too," Rob agreed.

They both left the restaurant five minutes later.

Chapter 50

As Rob drove home from his dinner with Lois, he prayed for her. He asked God to help her realize that He was still in control.

He thought it was interesting how perspectives on the same event could be so different. When Rob lost his father, he knew that he needed to cling to God and that he couldn't make it without Him. For Lois, she had gotten angry with God, blaming Him for her father's death. Rob prayed that her heart would be softened and that she would come back to faith in Christ.

Lois also thought about her evening as she drove home. She was surprised at how kind Rob was. Although Rob never mentioned it, Lois had the feeling that he would pray for her.

She looked down at her dashboard and saw that a red check engine light was glowing on the dashboard. *That's odd.* Lois thought. *I didn't notice it this morning.*

Soon she realized that her lights were growing dim and that her car started to slow. She swiftly pulled over on the side of the road.

She did it just in time. Just as she pulled over her engine shut off.

Lois's eyes slid shut in frustration. *So what do I do now?* Lois thought. *I'm miles away from home.*

A voice that she hardly remembered whispered one word. *Pray. Pray!* Lois thought to herself. *I haven't prayed in years.* Then she thought to herself that it wouldn't hurt anything.

God, Lois, started praying, *if You're real then please let the car start.*

Lois took a deep breath and turned the key in the ignition. To her surprise and pleasure the car started up without trouble.

She put on her blinker and entered the flow of traffic.

When she got home, she went inside and sat on her couch in the living room. God had proven Himself to be active in her daily life. She sat there and let it sink in. Why would God care about what happened to her? She had shut Him out of her life for so long.

Lois knew that she needed to get back on the right path. So, right there sitting on her couch she rededicated her life to Christ. When she finally surrendered she felt such relief and peace.

These were emotions she hadn't felt since her father died all those years ago. The next thing that Lois did was call her mom. It was past time to make things right.

Chicago

Sarah was at home praying for her daughter when the phone rang.

She answered on the third ring wondering who would be calling so late at night. "Hello."

"Hi Mom. Sorry that I'm calling so late," Lois said.

"That's all right. What's on your mind? I know this will sound strange, but I've been expecting your call."

Lois told her mom the whole thing from the beginning of her evening with Rob. She ended by saying, "I've had a change of heart. Tonight I gave my life back to God."

At this news, both mother and daughter cried tears of joy and release.

"I'm sorry Mom. I haven't been very nice to you these last couple of years," Lois said contritely. "Will you forgive me?"

"Of course I forgive you. You have no idea how long I've prayed for this moment."

The two talked for the next half hour and resolved some of their arguments from the past.

Lois was emotionally drained after she hung up the phone.

As she climbed into bed she suddenly remembered that she would need to charge her battery before leaving the next morning.

Since the only person that she knew was Rob, she called him.

"Hello?"

"Hi Rob, its Lois. I've got some car trouble. My car battery died, and I wondered if you have any jumper cables," Lois asked hesitantly, she didn't want to sound like a damsel in distress.

"Sure, I have jumper cables. I guess that I'll just find them and come on over," Rob said.

"Thanks Rob. Do you have my address?"

"Yes, I do. It was part of the paperwork that you filled out," Rob said after thinking for a moment.

Fifteen minutes later Rob arrived with the jumper cables.

While Lois waited for Rob, she stood by her window so that she would know when he got there.

When Rob knocked on the door, she opened it right away.

"Thanks for coming Rob. I'm quite embarrassed," Lois told him.

"There's nothing to be embarrassed about," Rob told her with sincerity. Then as they stepped out onto the front porch he asked, "Has your car been having a lot of problems recently?"

Lois shook her head no and proceeded to tell Rob about her change of heart. "I really think that God made my car break down. Does that sound ridiculous?"

"Not at all, you should read sometime about what God did to bring Saul to his senses. Seriously, though. I'm really happy for you." Rob said at the conclusion of her story.

By this time, Rob had finished hooking up the jumper cables to Lois's battery.

"Thanks," after pausing for a few seconds she said, "Would you mind if I call you in the morning if I have trouble again? I'm going to buy a new battery."

"Okay. That sounds good to me."

"All right. Thanks again Rob."

"You're welcome. Anytime you need help you're welcome to call. I don't promise I'll always be able to help, but you can always call me," Rob said trying to ease the awkwardness and embarrassment of their conversation. It worked. Lois smiled and said good night to Rob.

Chapter 51

Laura and Andy continued to do things together on a daily basis, and when they weren't together, they talked on the phone.

She went to his church on Sundays and continued to grow in her faith.

One Sunday afternoon Laura and Andy were having lunch together that Andy had prepared himself. He made mashed potatoes, fried chicken, and green beans.

They talked about everything under the sun.

"So, Laura do you think that you'll do more acting?" Andy asked at one point.

"I'd like to," Laura said with a nod.

Thoughts of acting made Laura think about Rob. It had been six months since she had been in Hollywood.

She hoped that he had been able to meet someone new and move on.

"I think I've lost you," Andy said with a compassionate smile.

"Oh, I'm sorry were you saying something?" Laura asked with a sheepish expression.

"I wondered if you had heard from Rob recently."

"No, I haven't heard from him in a while."

Andy started to say something but decided that now wasn't the time.

Laura looked at him quizzically but didn't say anything.

"Would you like some dessert?" Andy asked changing the mood.

"Sure. Do you need any help?" she asked.

"No, I'll get it."

While Andy was getting dessert, she thought about the past couple of months.

They had been spending a lot of time together. He seemed to be a bit different lately.

He was always doing things for her, always making her feel special. She realized how much she loved him. It was more than she could have imagined. Growing up together had allowed them to really get to know each other.

It was still on her mind when Andy came in with the dessert.

"Here you go. Would you like strawberry ice cream with your cake or would you like chocolate ice cream?" he asked carrying in both.

"I think that I'll take the strawberry," Laura said with anticipation.

It was her favorite dessert, a yellow cake with chocolate icing. She took a bite and was surprised that it tasted better than usual. "Is this homemade?" Laura asked.

Andy nodded as he took a bite. He swallowed and said, "It's my mom's recipe."

Laura was impressed with Andy's culinary skills.

They talked for several more hours. At around 4:30 Laura decided that it was time to get home.

"Thanks for lunch Andy. You're a great cook," Laura said as she was about to leave.

"You're welcome. Laura?" Andy said hesitantly.

"Yes?"

Andy had a hard time not getting down on one knee here and now. He loved her so much. He realized that he had to say something so that Laura wouldn't become suspicious. "I just have to tell you that you are the most amazing woman I have ever met."

"You really know how to melt a woman's heart," Laura said. "You are the most amazing man that I have ever met too."

After Laura left Andy thought to himself, *I have to ask her soon. I don't know how much longer I can wait to ask her to marry me.*

Chapter 52

Hollywood

As the filming wrapped up Rob, and Lois spent a lot of time together talking, praying, and doing things together.

They began dating soon after Lois turned back to God.

One day, about six months after they had started dating, Rob asked Lois, "Will you go to dinner with me tonight?"

"Yes, I'd love to go. What time should I be ready?" Lois asked with a cute smile.

"How about seven o'clock? Does that work ?"

Lois nodded. "Sounds good to me."

"All right. I'll see you then," Rob told her giving her a hug.

Rob was grateful that things hadn't worked out between Laura and himself. He and Lois connected in a way he had never connected with anyone else.

Lois decided to get very dressed up for her evening with Rob. She had a feeling that something very special was going to happen.

She loved Rob. She wanted to spend the rest of her life with him.

As she thought about him, he came to the door. "Hello Rob," Lois said as she opened the door.

"Hi Lois. These are for you," he said holding out a dozen long stemmed roses and a box of her favorite candy.

"Oh, thank you Rob. These are beautiful roses," she said. "I'll go put these in some water."

"You look great," Rob said as she came back out of her kitchen.

"Thank you Rob. You look great too."

"Shall we go?" he asked offering his arm.

"Sounds excellent."

When they got to the car Lois asked what restaurant they were going to.

Rob refused to tell her where they were heading.

Lois soon gave up on knowing where they were headed and just enjoyed being with the man she loved.

He seemed to be nervous today.

Lois was shocked when they pulled up in front of the fanciest restaurant in all of Hollywood.

"Rob!" Lois exclaimed.

"Yes?" Rob asked with a smile.

"Rob, this looks beautiful."

"Thank you. Let's go."

As they entered the restaurant, they heard soft romantic music and saw a large water feature with goldfish. In the middle of the water feature was a waterfall.

Rob and Lois were greeted by the maitre d'.

"Do you have a reservation?"

"Yes, Robert Lancing party of two."

After checking the reservation list, he led them to a private booth with plush seats. In the middle of the table was a beautiful bouquet of roses and wild flowers.

"Rob, I can't believe this. I've never been to a restaurant that was this fancy," Lois said after being seated.

"I hoped that you would like it," Rob said feeling pleased with himself.

Lois opened the menu and saw that there weren't any prices.

Rob watched her face, so he immediately said, "Don't worry about the cost. Order whatever you want."

He could tell that she was nervous, so he struck up a conversation in order to calm her nerves. It worked.

By the time, their drinks arrived she had relaxed and was enjoying the night.

At one point in the conversation Lois said, "It's hard to believe that I've only known you for eight months. I feel like I've known you much longer."

"I know what you mean. I feel like I've always known you. Lois I love you," Rob said. His heart was beating so fast that he was almost out of breath.

"I love you too," Lois said, her heart soaring.

They leaned toward each other and shared a tender kiss.

When they separated Rob took Lois' hand and asked, "Lois Anne McMurray will you marry me?"

At this point, he reached inside his suit coat and pulled out a velvet ring box.

Lois took the box with shaky hands. She opened it and gasped.

Inside was a beautiful gold engagement ring. There was a princess cut diamond in the middle and five diamonds in decreasing size on either side of it. She had never seen anything like it.

Rob gently took the ring from the box and put it on Lois' extended hand.

Lois suddenly realized that she hadn't said anything yet. So she quickly said, "Yes, yes I'll marry you!"

The rest of the night was a blur for both of them.

Epilogue

The next day was Saturday, so Rob didn't wake up until 10:30. He decided to skip breakfast and just wait to eat until lunch.

As he was doing his chores, the phone rang. Expecting it to be Lois he answered on the first ring.

"Hello."

"Hi Rob," a familiar voice said.

"Hi. Whom am I speaking to?" he asked afraid of making a blunder.

There was a laugh on the other end of the phone and he heard, "Its Laura. Has it been that long?" she asked, still chuckling.

"Hey Laura, it has been a while. How are you doing?" he asked wondering why she had called.

"I'm doing well. How about you?" she asked in return.

"I'm doing great."

"Listen Rob, I'll tell you why I called. I'm engaged to Andy. I wanted you to be the first to know," Laura said rapidly.

"How did he propose?" he asked.

"Well, he picked me up at around nine last Friday and took

me to breakfast at our favorite diner. Then we went and played miniature golf and watched a movie. After that, we went to the zoo and just spent the entire day together.

"To end the evening we went to a fancy restaurant. When he took me home, he asked me what part of the day had been my favorite. I told him I couldn't choose and then I asked what his favorite part was. His response was so sweet. He said 'My favorite part of the day was the fact that I got to spend it with you.'" Laura said in a dreamy tone. "Then he got down on one knee and said, Laura will you make every day my favorite day by becoming my wife? So of course I said yes."

"I'm glad that you called. I just got engaged as well," he told her.

Laura let out a relieved laugh and said, "Congratulations. I'm happy for you. Have you set a date yet?"

"We haven't set a date yet. I asked her last night," Rob told her with a smile in his voice.

"I'm glad that everything worked out, for both of us."

"Thanks. I am too."

"Well, I better be going. I wish both of you all the best that God has for you."

"Thanks Laura. I wish the same to you."

"Good-bye Rob," Laura said realizing this might be the last time she talked to him. Now that they were both getting married their lives would go in separate directions, but Laura couldn't have been happier that things had worked out this way. She loved Andy more than she could ever have imagined loving anyone. It made all the heart ache and tears worth it. She almost forgot that she was still on the phone until she heard Rob say, "Goodbye, Laura."

"Goodbye, Rob."

Seconds later they both hung up the phone and went about their days.

Before Rob continued with his chores, he realized that a weight had been lifted off his shoulders.

Thank you Lord for providing and taking care of us. You knew all along how this would work out, all along.

Laura was so happy and carefree at that moment that she just spun around in circles like a school girl.

Andy came in the door just then and just watched his wife-to-be. He couldn't imagine anything more perfect than this moment. He went to her and spun her into his embrace while she was in mid swing.

I was wrong; Andy thought as he looked into her eyes, *being in her arms is the most perfect place to be.*